The Short Cases of Inspector Maigret

In this intriguing collection are five of the great Inspector Maigret's shorter cases—appearing for the first time in book form. From the clatter and tumult of metropolitan Paris to the small villages of provincial France, these five adventures present an authentic and colorful picture of middle-class French life. And through them all moves the great sleuth himself—"slow, heavy, plodding, tormented, of inexhaustible patience, inextinguishable persistence"—who, whether he is holding a vicious killer at bay or pondering his latest lead in a peaceful bistro, remains one of the world's most *formidable* detectives. The five cases gathered here are:

Maigret's Christmas
Journey Backward into Time
Stan the Killer
The Old Lady of Bayeux
The Most Obstinate Man in Paris

Scene: France

These stories have appeared in *Ellery Queen's Mystery Magazine*.

By Georges Simenon

The Short Cases of

INSPECTOR MAIGRET

by Georges Simenon

S
D

Published for the Crime Club by
Doubleday & Company, Inc., Garden City, New York, 1959

All of the stories in this volume made their initial
American appearance in *Ellery Queen's Mystery Magazine*.

*All of the characters in this book are fictitious, and any resemblance
to actual persons, living or dead, is purely coincidental.*

Library of Congress Catalog Card Number 59–9788
Copyright © 1959 by Doubleday & Company, Inc.
Copyright © 1949, 1952, 1954, 1956, 1957 by Davis Publications, Inc.
(formerly Mercury Publications, Inc.)
All Rights Reserved
Printed in the United States of America
First Edition

Anthony Boucher introduces . . .

He is the most famous policeman in the fiction of Europe, and quite possibly of the world.

He has lost count, but thinks he has appeared in about fifty novels and at least as many shorter stories. (This is the first time that his briefer cases have appeared in book form in America.)

He is now around seventy-five and lives in retirement in Meung-sur-Loire, near Orléans (and not too far from Paris).

He was, in the 1920's and '30's and '40's, one of the greatest detectives of the Quai des Orfèvres (offices of the Judiciary Police).

Yet no one ever relied less on the scientific methodology for which the French police have been celebrated since Bertillon.

He detects by patience, by intuition, by a subtle understanding of criminal psychology, by an almost telepathic rapport with the minds of murderers.

As a young man he studied medicine for three years; perhaps to that training he owes some of his clinical insight into humanity.

He is the only detective who is demoted in translation. (In Paris he is a *commissaire; inspecteur* is a lower rank in the French police, comparable to the English and American *sergeant.*)

He seems, like many French actors, to have only a single name; his Christian name (Jules) is hardly ever mentioned. His wife's occurs even less frequently—and sometimes as Henriette, sometimes as Louise.

He is the only detective in fiction who has written and published an entire book (*Les Mémoires de Maigret*, 1950), in which he freely and often sharply criticizes his creator.

He has been played on the screen by actors as eminent and diverse as Harry Baur, Charles Laughton and Jean Gabin. (He himself thinks the best, or at least the most nearly like him, was Pierre Renoir.)

He has appeared in America by fits and starts—a few novels in 1932, a longer series in the early 1940's, and now, since 1953, a regular one or two books a year, as more and more Americans succumb to the fascination of his unconventional cases.

He is, *en somme*, the patient, the subtle, the indefatigable, the incomparable

MAIGRET

The Short Cases of Inspector Maigret

Maigret's Christmas

*T*HE ROUTINE NEVER VARIED. When Maigret went to bed he must have muttered his usual, "Tomorrow morning I shall sleep late." And Madame Maigret, who over the years should have learned to pay no attention to such casual phrases, had taken him at his word this Christmas Day.

It was not quite daylight when he heard her stirring cautiously. He forced himself to breathe regularly and deeply as though he were still asleep. It was like a game. She inched toward the edge of the bed with animal stealth, pausing after each movement to make sure she had not awakened him. He waited anxiously for the inevitable finale, the moment when the bedsprings, relieved of her weight, would rise back into place with a faint sigh.

She picked up her clothing from the chair and turned the knob of the bathroom door so slowly that it seemed to take an eternity. It was not until she had reached the distant fastness of the kitchen that she resumed her normal movements.

Maigret had fallen asleep again. Not deeply, nor for long. Long enough, however, for a confused and disturbing dream. Waking, he could not remember what it was, but he knew it was disturbing because he still felt vaguely uneasy.

The crack between the window drapes, which never quite closed, became a strip of pale, hard daylight. He waited a while longer, lying on his back with his eyes open, savoring the fragrance of fresh coffee. Then he heard the apartment door open and close, and he knew that Madame Maigret was hurrying downstairs to buy him hot *croissants* from the bakery at the corner of the Rue Amelot.

He never ate in the morning. His breakfast consisted of black coffee. But his wife clung to her ritual: on Sundays and holidays he was supposed to lie in bed until midmorning while she went out for *croissants*.

He got up, stepped into his slippers, put on his dressing gown, and drew the curtains. He knew he was doing wrong. His wife would be heartbroken. But while he was willing to make almost any sacrifice to please her, he just could not stay in bed longer than he felt like it.

It was not snowing. It was nonsense, of course, for a man past fifty to be disappointed because there was no snow on Christmas morning; but then middle-aged people never have as much sense as young folks sometimes imagine.

A dirty, turbid sky hung low over the rooftops. The Boulevard Richard Lenoir was completely deserted. The words *Fils et Cie.*, *Bonded Warehouses*, on the sign above the porte-cochere across the street, stood out as black as mourning crepe. The *F*, for some strange reason, seemed particularly dismal.

He heard his wife moving about in the kitchen again. She came into the dining room on tiptoe, as though he were still asleep instead of looking out the window. He glanced at his watch on the night table. It was only ten past eight.

The night before the Maigrets had gone to the theater. They would have loved dropping in for a snack at some restaurant, like everyone else on Christmas Eve, but all tables were reserved for

Réveillon supper. So they had walked home arm in arm, getting in a few minutes before midnight. So they hadn't long to wait before exchanging presents.

He got a pipe, as usual. Her present was an electric coffeepot, the latest model that she had wanted so much, and, not to break with tradition, a dozen finely embroidered handkerchiefs.

Still looking out the window, Maigret absently filled his new pipe. The shutters were still closed on some of the windows across the boulevard. Not many people were up. Here and there a light burned in a window, probably left by children who had leaped out of bed at the crack of dawn to rush for their presents under the Christmas tree.

In the quiet Maigret apartment the morning promised to be a lazy one for just the two of them. Maigret would loiter in his dressing gown until quite late. He would not even shave. He would dawdle in the kitchen, talking to his wife while she put the lunch on the stove. Just the two of them.

He wasn't melancholy exactly, but his dream—which he couldn't remember—had left him jumpy. Or perhaps it wasn't his dream. Perhaps it was Christmas. He had to be extra careful on Christmas Day, careful of his words, the way Madame Maigret had been careful of her movements in getting out of bed. Her nerves, too, were especially sensitive on Christmas.

Oh well, why think of all that? He would just be careful to say nothing untoward. He would be careful not to look out of the window when the neighborhood children began to appear on the sidewalks with their Christmas toys.

All the houses in the street had children. Or almost all. The street would soon echo to the shrill blast of toy horns, the roll of toy drums, and the crack of toy pistols. The little girls were probably already cradling their new dolls.

A few years ago he had proposed more or less at random: "Why don't we take a little trip for Christmas?"

"Where?" she had replied with her infallible common sense.

Where, indeed? Whom would they visit? They had no relatives

except her sister, who lived too far away. And why spend Christmas in some second-rate country hotel, or in a hotel in some strange town?

Oh well, he'd feel better after he had his coffee. He was never at his best until he'd drunk his first cup of coffee and lit his first pipe.

Just as he was reaching for the knob, the door opened noiselessly and Madame Maigret appeared carrying a tray. She looked at the empty bed, then turned her disappointed eyes upon her husband. She was on the verge of tears.

"You got up!" She looked as though she had been up for hours herself, every hair in place, a picture of neatness in her crisp clean apron. "And I was so happy about serving your breakfast in bed."

He had tried a hundred times, as subtly as he could, to make her understand that he didn't like eating breakfast in bed. It made him uncomfortable. It made him feel like an invalid or a senile old gaffer. But for Madame Maigret breakfast in bed was the symbol of leisure and luxury, the ideal way to start Sunday or a holiday.

"Don't you want to go back to bed?"

No, he did not. Decidedly not. He hadn't the courage.

"Then come to breakfast in the kitchen. And Merry Christmas."

"Merry Christmas! . . . You're not angry?"

They were in the dining room. He surveyed the silver tray on a corner of the table, the steaming cup of coffee, the golden-brown *croissants*. He put down his pipe and ate a *croissant* to please his wife, but he remained standing, looking out the window.

"It's snowing."

It wasn't real snow. It was a fine white dust sifting down from the sky, but it reminded Maigret that when he was a small boy he used to stick out his tongue to lick up a few of the tiny flakes.

His gaze focused on the entrance to the building across the street, next door to the warehouse. Two women had just come out, both bareheaded. One of them, a blonde of about thirty, had thrown a coat over her shoulders without stopping to slip her arms into the sleeves. The other, a brunette, older and thinner, was hugging a shawl.

The blonde seemed to hesitate, ready to turn back. Her slim little companion was insistent and Maigret had the impression that she was pointing up toward his window. The appearance of the concierge in the doorway behind them seemed to tip the scales in favor of the little brunette. The blonde looked back apprehensively, then crossed the street.

"What are you looking at?"

"Nothing . . . two women. . . ."

"What are they doing?"

"I think they're coming here."

The two women had stopped in the middle of the street and were looking up in the direction of the Maigret apartment.

"I hope they're not coming here to bother you on Christmas Day. My housework's not even done." Nobody would have guessed it. There wasn't a speck of dust on any of the polished furniture. "Are you sure they're coming here?"

"We'll soon find out."

To be on the safe side, he went to comb his hair, brush his teeth, and splash a little water on his face. He was still in his room, relighting his pipe, when he heard the doorbell. Madame Maigret was evidently putting up a strong hedgehog defense, for it was some time before she came for him.

"They insist on talking to you," she whispered. "They claim it's very important and they need advice. I know one of them."

"Which one?"

"The skinny little one, Mademoiselle Doncoeur. She lives across the street on the same floor as ours. She's a very nice person and she does embroidery for a firm in the Faubourg Saint Honoré. I sometimes wonder if she isn't in love with you."

"Why?"

"Because she works near the window, and when you leave the

house in the morning she sometimes gets up to watch you go down the street."

"How old is she?"

"Forty-five to fifty. Aren't you getting dressed?"

Doesn't a man have the right to lounge in his dressing gown, even if people come to bother him at eight-thirty on Christmas morning? Well, he'd compromise. He'd put his trousers on underneath the robe.

The two women were standing when he walked into the dining room.

"Excuse me, mesdames . . ."

Perhaps Madame Maigret was right. Mademoiselle Doncoeur did not blush; she paled, smiled, lost her smile, smiled again. She opened her mouth to speak but said nothing.

The blonde, on the other hand, was perfectly composed. She said with a touch of humor, "Coming here wasn't my idea."

"Won't you sit down?"

Maigret noticed that the blonde was wearing a house dress under her coat and that her legs were bare. Mademoiselle Doncoeur was dressed as though for church.

"You perhaps wonder at our boldness in coming to you like this," Mademoiselle Doncoeur said finally, choosing her words carefully. "Like everyone in the neighborhood, we are honored to have such a distinguished neighbor. . . ." She paused, blushed, and stared at the tray. "We're keeping you from your breakfast."

"I've finished. I'm at your service."

"Something happened in our building last night, or rather this morning, which was so unusual that I felt it was our duty to speak to you about it immediately. Madame Martin did not want to disturb you, but I told her——"

"You also live across the street, Madame Martin?"

"Yes, monsieur." Madame Martin was obviously unhappy at being forced to take this step. Mademoiselle Doncoeur, however, was now fully wound up.

"We live on the same floor, just across from your windows."

She blushed again, as if she were making a confession. "Monsieur Martin is often out of town, which is natural enough since he is a traveling salesman. For the past two months their little girl has been in bed, as a result of a silly accident. . . ."

Maigret turned politely to the blonde. "You have a daughter?"

"Well, not a daughter exactly. She's our niece. Her mother died two years ago and she's been living with us ever since. The girl broke her leg on the stairs. She should have been up and about after six weeks, but there were complications."

"Your husband is on the road at present?"

"He should be in Bergerac."

"I'm listening, Mademoiselle Doncoeur."

Madame Maigret had detoured through the bathroom to regain the kitchen. The clatter of pots and pans had resumed. Maigret stared through the window at the leaden sky.

"I got up early this morning as usual," said Mademoiselle Doncoeur, "to go to first Mass."

"And you did go to church?"

"Yes. I stayed for three Masses. I got home about seven-thirty and made my breakfast. You may have seen the light in my window."

Maigret's gesture indicated that he had not been watching.

"I was in a hurry to take a few goodies to Colette. It's very sad for a child to spend Christmas in bed. Colette is Madame Martin's niece."

"How old is she?"

"Seven. Isn't that right, Madame Martin?"

"She'll be seven in January."

"So at eight o'clock I knocked at the door of their apartment——"

"I wasn't up," the blonde interrupted. "I sometimes sleep rather late."

"As I was saying, I knocked. Madame Martin kept me waiting for a moment while she slipped on her negligee. I had my arms full, and I asked if I could take my presents in to Colette."

Maigret noted that the blonde was making a mental inventory of the apartment, stopping occasionally to dart a sharp, suspicious glance in his direction.

"We opened the door to her room together——"

"The child has a room of her own?"

"Yes. There are two bedrooms in the apartment, a dressing room, a kitchen, and a dining room. But I must tell you—— No, I'm getting ahead of myself. We had just opened the door and, since the room was dark, Madame Martin had switched on the light——"

"Colette was awake?"

"Yes. It was easy to see she'd been awake for some time, waiting. You know how children are on Christmas morning. If she could use her legs, she would certainly have got up long since to see what Father Christmas had brought her. Perhaps another child would have called out. But Colette is already a little lady. She's much older than her age. She thinks a lot."

Now Madame Martin was looking out the window. Maigret tried to guess which apartment was hers. It must be the last one to the right, the one with the two lighted windows.

"I wished her a Merry Christmas," Mademoiselle Doncoeur continued. "I said to her, and these were my exact words, 'Darling, look what Father Christmas left in my apartment for you.'"

Madame Martin was clasping and unclasping her fingers.

"And do you know what she answered me, without even looking to see what I'd brought? They were only trifles, anyhow. She said, 'I saw him.'"

"'Whom did you see?'"

"'Father Christmas.'"

"'When did you see him?' I asked. 'Where?'"

"'Right here, last night. He came to my room.'"

"That's exactly what she said, isn't it, Madame Martin? With any other child, we would have smiled. But as I told you, Colette is already a little lady. She doesn't joke. I said, 'How could you see him, since it was dark?'"

" 'He had a light.'

" 'You mean he turned on the electricity?'

" 'No. He had a flashlight. Look, Mamma Loraine.'

"I must tell you that the little girl calls Madame Martin 'Mamma,' which is natural enough, since her own mother is dead and Madame Martin has been taking her place."

The monologue had become a confused buzzing in Maigret's ears. He had not drunk his second cup of coffee and his pipe had gone out. He asked without conviction, "Did she really see someone?"

"Yes, Monsieur l'Inspecteur. And that's why I insisted that Madame Martin come to speak to you. Colette did see someone and she proved it to us. With a sly little smile she threw back the bed sheet and showed us a magnificent doll . . . a beautiful big doll she was cuddling and I swear was not in the house yesterday."

"You didn't give your niece a doll, Madame Martin?"

"I was going to give her one, but mine was not nearly as nice. I got it yesterday afternoon at the Galeries, and I was holding it behind me this morning when we came into her room."

"In other words, someone *did* come into your apartment last night?"

"That's not all," said Mademoiselle Doncoeur quickly; she was not to be stopped. "Colette never tells lies. She's not a child who imagines things. And when we questioned her, she said the man was certainly Father Christmas because he wore a white beard and a bright red coat."

"At what time did she wake up?"

"She doesn't know—sometime during the night. She opened her eyes because she thought she saw a light. And there was a light, shining on the floor near the fireplace."

"I can't understand it," sighed Madame Martin. "Unless my husband has some explanation . . ."

But Mademoiselle Doncoeur was not to be diverted from her story. It was obvious that she was the one who had questioned the child, just as she was the one who had thought of Maigret. She resumed:

"Colette said, 'Father Christmas was squatting on the floor, and he was bending over, as if he were working at something.' "

"She wasn't frightened?"

"No. She just watched him. This morning she told us he was busy making a hole in the floor. She thought he wanted to go through the floor to visit the people downstairs—that's the Delormes, who have a little boy of three—because the chimney was too narrow. The man must have sensed she was watching him, because he got up, came over to the bed, and gave Colette the big doll. Then he put his finger to his lips."

"Did she see him leave?"

"Yes."

"Through the floor?"

"No, by the door."

"Into what room does this door open?"

"Directly into the outside hall. There is another door that opens into the apartment, but the hall door is like a private entrance because the room used to be rented separately."

"Wasn't the door locked?"

"Of course," Madame Martin intervened. "I wouldn't let the child sleep in a room that wasn't locked from the outside."

"Then the door was forced?"

"Probably. I don't know. Mademoiselle Doncoeur immediately suggested we come to see you."

"Did you find a hole in the floor?"

Madame Martin shrugged wearily, but Mademoiselle Doncoeur answered for her.

"Not a hole exactly, but you could see that the floor boards had been moved."

"Tell me, Madame Martin, have you any idea what might have been hidden under the flooring?"

"No, monsieur."

"How long have you lived in this apartment?"

"Since my marriage, five years ago."

"And this room was part of the apartment then?"

"Yes."

"You know who lived there before you?"

"My husband. He's thirty-eight. He was thirty-three when we were married, and he had his own furniture then. He liked to have his own home to come back to when he returned to Paris from the road."

"Do you think he might have wanted to surprise Colette?"

"He is six or seven hundred kilometers from here."

"Where did you say?"

"In Bergerac. His itinerary is planned in advance and he rarely deviates from his schedule."

"For what firm does he travel?"

"He covers the central and southwest territory for Zenith watches. It's an important line, as you probably know. He has a very good job."

"There isn't a finer man on earth!" exclaimed Mademoiselle Doncoeur. She blushed, then added, "Except you, Monsieur l'Inspecteur."

"As I understand it then, someone got into your apartment last night disguised as Father Christmas."

"According to the little girl."

"Didn't you hear anything? Is your room far from the little girl's?"

"There's the dining room between us."

"Don't you leave the connecting doors open at night?"

"It isn't necessary. Colette is not afraid, and as a rule she never wakes up. If she wants anything, she has a little bell on her night table."

"Did you go out last night?"

"I did not, Monsieur l'Inspecteur." Madame Martin was annoyed.

"Did you receive visitors?"

"I do not receive visitors while my husband is away."

Maigret glanced at Mademoiselle Doncoeur, whose expression did not change. So Madame Martin was telling the truth.

"Did you go to bed late?"

"I read until midnight. As soon as the radio played 'Minuit, Chrétiens,' I went to bed."

"And you heard nothing unusual?"

"Nothing."

"Have you asked the concierge if she clicked the latch to let in any strangers last night?"

"I asked her," Mademoiselle Doncoeur volunteered. "She says she didn't."

"And you found nothing missing from your apartment this morning, Madame Martin? Nothing disturbed in the dining room?"

"No."

"Who is with the little girl now?"

"No one. She's used to staying alone. I can't be at home all day. I have marketing to do, errands to run. . . ."

"I understand. You told me Colette is an orphan?"

"Her mother is dead."

"So her father is living. Where is he?"

"Her father's name is Paul Martin. He's my husband's brother. As to telling you where he is——" Madame Martin sketched a vague gesture.

"When did you see him last?"

"About a month ago. A little longer. It was around All Saints' Day. He was finishing a novena."

"I beg your pardon?"

"I may as well tell you everything at once," said Madame Martin with a faint smile, "since we seem to be washing our family linen." She glanced reproachfully at Mademoiselle Doncoeur. "My brother-in-law, especially since he lost his wife, is not quite respectable."

"What do you mean exactly?"

"He drinks. He always drank a little, but he never used to get into trouble. He had a good job with a furniture store in the Faubourg Saint Antoine. But since the accident . . ."

"The accident to his daughter?"

"No, to his wife. He borrowed a car from a friend one Sunday about three years ago and took his wife and little girl to the country. They had lunch at a roadside inn near Mantes la Jolie and he drank too much white wine. He sang most of the way back to Paris—until he ran into something near the Bougival bridge. His wife was killed instantly. He cracked his own skull and it's a miracle he's still alive. Colette escaped without a scratch. Paul hasn't been a man since then. We've practically adopted the little girl. He comes to see her occasionally when he's sober. Then he starts over again. . . ."

"Do you know where he lives?"

Another vague gesture. "Everywhere. We've seen him loitering around the Bastille like a beggar. Sometimes he sells papers in the street. I can speak freely in front of Mademoiselle Doncoeur because unfortunately the whole house knows about him."

"Don't you think he might have dressed up as Father Christmas to call on his daughter?"

"That's what I told Mademoiselle Doncoeur, but she insisted on coming to see you anyhow."

"Because I see no reason for him to take up the flooring," said Mademoiselle Doncoeur acidly.

"Or perhaps your husband returned to Paris unexpectedly. . . ."

"It's certainly something of the sort. I'm not at all disturbed. But Mademoiselle Doncoeur——"

Decidedly Madame Martin had not crossed the boulevard lightheartedly.

"Do you know where your husband might be staying in Bergerac?"

"Yes. At the Hôtel de Bordeaux."

"You hadn't thought of telephoning him?"

"We have no phone. There's only one in the house—the people on the second floor, and they hate to be disturbed."

"Would you object to my calling the Hôtel de Bordeaux?"

Madame Martin started to nod, then hesitated. "He'll think something terrible has happened."

"You can speak to him yourself."

"He's not used to my phoning him on the road."

"You'd rather he not know what's happening?"

"That's not so. I'll talk to him if you like."

Maigret picked up the phone and placed the call. Ten minutes later he was connected with the Hôtel de Bordeaux in Bergerac. He passed the instrument to Madame Martin.

"Hello . . . Monsieur Martin, please . . . Yes, Monsieur Jean Martin. . . . It doesn't matter. Wake him up."

She put her hand over the mouthpiece. "He's still asleep. They've gone to call him."

Then she retreated into silence, evidently rehearsing the words she was to speak to her husband.

"Hello? . . . Hello, darling . . . What? . . . Yes, Merry Christmas! . . . Yes, everything's all right . . . Colette is fine . . . No, that's not why I phoned . . . No, no, no! Nothing's wrong. Please don't worry!" She repeated each word separately. "Please . . . don't . . . worry! I just want to tell you about a strange thing that happened last night. Somebody dressed up like Father Christmas and came into Colette's room . . . No, no! He didn't hurt her. He gave her a big doll . . . Yes, *doll!* . . . And he did strange things to the floor. He removed two boards which he put back in a hurry . . . Mademoiselle Doncoeur thought I should report it to the police inspector who lives across the street. I'm there now . . . You don't understand? Neither do I . . . You want to talk to him?" She passed the instrument to Maigret. "He wants to speak to you."

A warm masculine voice came over the wire, the voice of an anxious, puzzled man.

"Are you sure my wife and the little girl are all right? . . . It's all so incredible! If it were just the doll, I might suspect my brother. Loraine will tell you about him. Loraine is my wife.

Ask her . . . But he wouldn't have removed the flooring . . . Do you think I'd better come home? I can get a train for Paris at three this afternoon . . . What? . . . Thank you so much. It's good to know you'll look after them."

Loraine Martin took back the phone.

"See, darling? The inspector says there's no danger. It would be foolish to break your trip now. It might spoil your chances of being transferred permanently to Paris. . . ."

Mademoiselle Doncoeur was watching her closely and there was little tenderness in the spinster's eyes.

". . . I promise to wire you or phone you if there's anything new . . . She's playing quietly with her new doll . . . No, I haven't had time yet to give her your present. I'll go right home and do it now."

Madame Martin hung up and declared, "You see." Then, after a pause, "Forgive me for bothering you. It's really not my fault. I'm sure this is all the work of some practical joker . . . unless it's my brother-in-law. When he's been drinking there's no telling what he might do."

"Do you expect to see him today? Don't you think he might want to see his daughter?"

"That depends. If he's been drinking, no. He's very careful never to come around in that condition."

"May I have your permission to come over and talk with Colette a little later?"

"I see no reason why you shouldn't—if you think it worth while. . . ."

"Thank you, Monsieur Maigret!" exclaimed Mademoiselle Doncoeur. Her expression was half grateful, half conspiratorial. "She's such an interesting child! You'll see!"

She backed toward the door.

A few minutes later Maigret watched the two women cross the boulevard. Mademoiselle Doncoeur, close on the heels of Madame Martin, turned to look up at the windows of the Maigret apartment.

Madame Maigret opened the kitchen door, flooding the dining room with the aroma of browning onions. She asked gently:

"Are you happy?"

He pretended not to understand. Luckily he had been too busy to think much about the middle-aged couple who had nobody to make a fuss over this Christmas morning.

It was time for him to shave and call on Colette.

HE WAS JUST ABOUT to lather his face when he decided to make a phone call. He didn't bother with his dressing gown. Clad only in pajamas, he dropped into the easy chair by the window—*his* chair—and watched the smoke curling up from all the chimney pots while his call went through.

The ringing at the other end—in headquarters at the Quai des Orfèvres—had a different sound from all other rings. It evoked for him the long empty corridors, the vacant offices, the operator stuck with holiday duty at the switchboard. . . . Then he heard the operator call Lucas with the words: "The boss wants you."

He felt a little like one of his wife's friends who could imagine no greater joy—which she experienced daily—than lying in bed all morning, with her windows closed and curtains drawn, and telephoning all her friends, one after the other. By the soft glow of her night light she managed to maintain a constant state of just having awakened. "What? Ten o'clock already? How's the weather? Is it raining? Have you been out yet? Have you done all your marketing?" And as she established telephonic connection with the hurly-burly of the workaday world, she would sink more and more voluptuously into the warm softness of her bed.

"That you, Chief?"

Maigret, too, felt a need for contact with the working world. He wanted to ask Lucas who was on duty with him, what they were doing, how the shop looked on this Christmas morning.

"Nothing new? Not too busy?"

"Nothing to speak of. Routine. . . ."

"I'd like you to get me some information. You can probably do this by phone. First of all, I want a list of all convicts released from prison the last two or three months."

"Which prison?"

"All prisons. But don't bother with any who haven't served at least five years. Then check and see if any of them have ever lived on Boulevard Richard Lenoir. Got that?"

"I'm making notes."

Lucas was probably somewhat bewildered, but he would never admit it.

"Another thing. I want you to locate a man named Paul Martin, a drunk, no fixed address, who frequently hangs out around the Place de la Bastille. I don't want him arrested. I don't want him molested. I just want to know where he spent Christmas Eve. The commissariats should help you on this one."

No use trying. Maigret simply could not reproduce the idle mood of his wife's friend. On the contrary, it embarrassed him to be lolling at home in his pajamas, unshaven, phoning from his favorite easy chair, looking out at a scene of complete peace and quiet in which there was no movement except the smoke rising from the chimneys, while at the other end of the line good old Lucas had been on duty since six in the morning and was probably already unwrapping his sandwiches.

"That's not quite all, old man. I want you to call Bergerac long distance. There's a traveling salesman by the name of Jean Martin staying at the Hôtel de Bordeaux there. No, Jean. It's his brother. I want to know if Jean Martin got a telegram or a phone call from Paris last night or any time yesterday. And while you're about it, find out where he spent Christmas Eve. I think that's all."

"Shall I call you back?"

"Not right away. I've got to go out for a while. I'll call you when I get home."

"Something happen in your neighborhood?"

"I don't know yet. Maybe."

Madame Maigret came into the bathroom to talk to him while he finished dressing. He did not put on his overcoat. The smoke curling slowly upward from so many chimneys blended with the gray of the sky and conjured up the image of just as many over-heated apartments, cramped rooms in which he would not be invited to make himself at home. He refused to be uncomfortable. He would put on his hat to cross the boulevard, and that was all.

The building across the way was very much like the one he lived in—old but clean, a little dreary, particularly on a drab December morning. He didn't stop at the concierge's lodge, but noted that she watched him with some annoyance. Doors opened silently as he climbed the stairs. He heard whispering, the padding of slippered feet.

Mademoiselle Doncoeur, who had doubtless been watching for him, was waiting on the fourth-floor landing. She was both shy and excited, as if keeping a secret tryst with a lover.

"This way, Monsieur Maigret. She went out a little while ago."

He frowned, and she noted the fact.

"I told her that you were coming and that she had better wait for you, but she said she had not done her marketing yesterday and that there was nothing in the house. She said all the stores would be closed if she waited too long. Come in."

She had opened the door into Madame Martin's dining room, a small, rather dark room that was clean and tidy.

"I'm looking after the little girl until she comes back. I told Colette that you were coming to see her, and she is delighted. I've spoken to her about you. She's only afraid you might take back her doll."

"When did Madame Martin decide to go out?"

"As soon as we came back across the street, she started dressing."

"Did she dress completely?"

"I don't understand."

"I mean, I suppose she dresses differently when she goes downtown than when she merely goes shopping in the neighborhood."

"She was quite dressed up. She put on her hat and gloves. And she carried her shopping bag."

Before going to see Colette, Maigret stepped into the kitchen and glanced at the breakfast dishes.

"Did she eat before you came to see me?"

"No. I didn't give her a chance."

"And when she came back?"

"She just made herself a cup of black coffee. I fixed breakfast for Colette while Madame Martin got dressed."

There was a cooler on the ledge of the window looking out on the courtyard. Maigret carefully examined its contents: butter, eggs, vegetables, some cold meat. He found two uncut loaves of fresh bread in the kitchen cupboard. Colette had eaten *croissants* with her hot chocolate.

"How well do you know Madame Martin?"

"We're neighbors, aren't we? And I've seen more of her since Colette has been in bed. She often asks me to keep an eye on the little girl when she goes out."

"Does she go out much?"

"Not very often. Just for her marketing."

Maigret tried to analyze the curious impression he had had on entering the apartment. There was something in the atmosphere that disturbed him, something about the arrangement of the furniture, the special kind of neatness that prevailed, even the smell of the place. As he followed Mademoiselle Doncoeur into the dining room, he thought that he knew what it was.

Madame Martin had told him that her husband had lived in this apartment before their marriage. And even though Madame Martin had lived there for five years, it had remained a bachelor's apartment. He pointed to the two enlarged photographs standing on opposite ends of the mantelpiece.

"Who are they?"

"Monsieur Martin's father and mother."

"Doesn't Madame Martin have photos of her own parents about?"

"I've never heard her speak of them. I suppose she's an orphan."

Even the bedroom was without the feminine touch. He opened a closet. Next to the neat rows of masculine clothing the woman's clothes were hanging, mostly severely tailored suits and conservative dresses. He did not open the bureau drawers but he was sure that they did not contain the usual trinkets and knickknacks that women collect.

"Mademoiselle Doncoeur!" called a calm little voice.

"Let's talk to Colette," said Maigret.

The child's room was as austere and cold as the others. The little girl lay in a bed too large for her, her face solemn, her eyes questioning but trusting.

"Are you the inspector, monsieur?"

"I'm the inspector, my girl. Don't be afraid."

"I'm not afraid. Hasn't Mamma Loraine come home yet?"

Maigret pursed his lips. The Martins had practically adopted their niece, yet the child said "Mamma Loraine," not just "Mamma."

"Do you believe it was Father Christmas who came to see me last night?" Colette asked Maigret.

"I'm sure it was."

"Mamma Loraine doesn't believe it. She never believes me."

The girl had a dainty, attractive little face, with very bright eyes that stared at Maigret with level persistence. The plaster cast that sheathed one leg all the way to the hip made a thick bulge under the blankets.

Mademoiselle Doncoeur hovered in the doorway, evidently anxious to leave the inspector alone with the girl. She said, "I must run home for a moment to make sure my lunch isn't burning."

Maigret sat down beside the bed, wondering how to go about questioning the girl.

"Do you love Mamma Loraine very much?" he began.

"Yes, monsieur." She replied without hesitation and without enthusiasm.

"And your papa?"

"Which one? Because I have two papas, you know—Papa Paul and Papa Jean."

"Has it been a long time since you saw Papa Paul?"

"I don't remember. Perhaps several weeks. He promised to bring me a toy for Christmas, but he hasn't come yet. He must be sick."

"Is he often sick?"

"Yes, often. When he's sick he doesn't come to see me."

"And your Papa Jean?"

"He's away on a trip, but he'll be back for New Year's. Maybe then he'll be appointed to the Paris office and won't have to go away any more. That would make him very happy, and me too."

"Do many of your friends come to see you since you've been in bed?"

"What friends? The girls in school don't know where I live. Or maybe they know but their parents don't let them come alone."

"What about Mamma Loraine's friends? Or your papa's?"

"Nobody comes, ever."

"Ever? Are you sure?"

"Only the man to read the gas meter, or for the electricity. I can hear them, because the door is almost always open. I recognize their voices. Once a man came and I didn't recognize his voice. Or twice."

"How long ago was that?"

"The first time was the day after my accident. I remember because the doctor just left."

"Who was it?"

"I didn't see him. He knocked at the other door. I heard him talking and then Mamma Loraine came and closed my door. They talked for quite a while but I couldn't hear very well. Afterward Mamma Loraine said it was a man who wanted to sell her some insurance. I don't know what that is."

"And he came back?"

"Five or six days ago. It was night and I'd already turned off my light. I wasn't asleep, though. I heard someone knock, and then they talked in low voices like the first time. Mademoiselle Doncoeur sometimes comes over in the evening, but I could tell it wasn't she. I thought they were quarreling and I was frightened. I called out, and Mamma Loraine came in and said it was the man about the insurance again and I should go to sleep."

"Did he stay long?"

"I don't know. I think I fell asleep."

"And you didn't see him either time?"

"No, but I'd recognize his voice."

"Even though he speaks in low tones?"

"Yes, that's why. When he speaks low it sounds just like a big bumblebee. I can keep the doll, can't I? Mamma Loraine bought me two boxes of candy and a little sewing kit. She bought me a doll, too, but it wasn't nearly as big as the doll Father Christmas gave me, because she's not rich. She showed it to me this morning before she left, and then she put it back in the box. I have the big one now, so I won't need the little one and Mamma Loraine can take it back to the store."

The apartment was overheated, yet Maigret felt suddenly cold. The building was very much like the one across the street, yet not only did the rooms seem smaller and stuffier, but the whole world seemed smaller and meaner over here.

He bent over the floor near the fireplace. He lifted the loose floor boards but saw nothing but an empty, dusty cavity smelling of dampness. There were scratches on the planks which indicated that they had been forced up with a chisel or some similar instrument.

He examined the outside door and found indications that it had been forced. It was obviously an amateur's work, and, luckily for him, the job had been an easy one.

"Father Christmas wasn't angry when he saw you watching him?"

"No, monsieur. He was busy making a hole in the floor so he could go and see the little boy downstairs."

"Did he speak to you?"

"I think he smiled at me. I'm not sure, though, because of his whiskers. It wasn't very light. But I'm sure he put his fingers to his lips so I wouldn't call anybody, because grownups aren't supposed to see Father Christmas. Did you ever see him?"

"A very long time ago."

"When you were little?"   **1069977**

Maigret heard footsteps in the hallway. The door opened and Madame Martin came in. She was wearing a gray tailored suit and a small beige hat and carried a brown shopping bag. She was visibly cold, for her skin was taut and very white, yet she must have hurried up the stairs, since there were two pink spots on her cheeks and she was out of breath. Unsmiling, she asked Maigret:

"Has she been a good girl?" Then, as she took off her jacket, "I apologize for making you wait. I had so many things to buy, and I was afraid the stores would all be closed later on."

"Did you meet anyone?"

"What do you mean?"

"Nothing. I was wondering if anyone tried to speak to you."

She had had plenty of time to go much farther than the Rue Amelot or the Rue du Chemin Vert, where most of the neighborhood shops were located. She had even had time to go across Paris and back by taxi or the Métro.

Mademoiselle Doncoeur returned to ask if there were anything she could do. Madame Martin was about to say no when Maigret intervened: "I'd like you to stay with Colette while I step into the next room."

Mademoiselle Doncoeur understood that he wanted her to keep the child busy while he questioned the foster mother. Madame Martin must have understood too, but she gave no indication.

"Please come in. Do you mind if I take off my things?"

Madame Martin put her packages in the kitchen. She took off her hat and fluffed out her pale blond hair. When she had closed the bedroom door, she said, "Mademoiselle Doncoeur is all excited.

This is quite an event, isn't it, for an old maid—particularly an old maid who cuts out every newspaper article about a certain police inspector, and who finally has the inspector in her own house. . . . Do you mind?"

She had taken a cigarette from a silver case, tapped the end, and snapped a lighter. The gesture somehow prompted Maigret's next question:

"You're not working, Madame Martin?"

"It would be difficult to hold a job and take care of the house and the little girl too, even when the child is in school. Besides, my husband won't allow me to work."

"But you did work before you met him?"

"Naturally. I had to earn a living. Won't you sit down?"

He lowered himself into a rude raffia-bottomed chair. She rested one thigh against the edge of a table.

"You were a typist?"

"I have been a typist."

"For long?"

"Quite a while."

"You were still a typist when you met Martin? You must forgive me for asking these personal questions."

"It's your job."

"You were married five years ago. Were you working then? Just a moment. May I ask your age?"

"I'm thirty-three. I was twenty-eight then, and I was working for a Monsieur Lorilleux in the Palais Royal arcades."

"As his secretary?"

"Monsieur Lorilleux had a jewelry shop. Or more exactly, he sold souvenirs and old coins. You know those old shops in the Palais Royal. I was salesgirl, bookkeeper, *and* secretary. I took care of the shop when he was away."

"He was married?"

"And father of three children."

"You left him to marry Martin?"

"Not exactly. Jean didn't want me to go on working, but he

wasn't making very much money then and I had quite a good job. So I kept it for the first few months."

"And then?"

"Then a strange thing happened. One morning I came to work at nine o'clock as usual, and I found the door locked. I thought Monsieur Lorilleux had overslept, so I waited. . . ."

"Where did he live?"

"Rue Mazarine with his family. At half past nine I began to worry."

"Was he dead?"

"No. I phoned his wife, who said he had left the house at eight o'clock as usual."

"Where did you telephone from?"

"From the glove shop next door. I waited all morning. His wife came down and we went to the commissariat together to report him missing, but the police didn't take it very seriously. They just asked his wife if he'd ever had heart trouble, if he had a mistress—things like that. But he was never seen again, and nobody ever heard from him. Then some Polish people bought out the store and my husband made me stop working."

"How long was this after your marriage?"

"Four months."

"Your husband was already traveling in the southwest?"

"He had the same territory he has now."

"Was he in Paris when your employer disappeared?"

"No, I don't think so."

"Didn't the police examine the premises?"

"Nothing had been touched since the night before. Nothing was missing."

"Do you know what became of Madame Lorilleux?"

"She lived for a while on the money from the sale of the store. Then she bought a little dry-goods shop not far from here, on the Rue du Pas de la Mule. Her children must be grown up now, probably married."

"Do you still see her?"

"I go into her shop once in a while. That's how I know she's in business in the neighborhood. The first time I saw her there I didn't recognize her."

"How long ago was that?"

"I don't know. Six months or so."

"Does she have a telephone?"

"I don't know. Why?"

"What kind of man was Lorilleux?"

"You mean physically?"

"Let's start with the physical."

"He was a big man, taller than you, and broader. He was fat, but flabby, if you know what I mean. And rather sloppy-looking."

"How old?"

"Around fifty. I can't say exactly. He had a little salt-and-pepper mustache, and his clothes were always too big for him."

"You were familiar with his habits?"

"He walked to work every morning. He got down fifteen minutes ahead of me and cleared up the mail before I arrived. He didn't talk much. He was a rather gloomy person. He spent most of the day in the little office behind the shop."

"No romantic adventures?"

"Not that I know of."

"Didn't he try to make love to you?"

"No!" The monosyllable was tartly emphatic.

"But he thought highly of you?"

"I think I was a great help to him."

"Did your husband ever meet him?"

"They never spoke. Jean sometimes came to wait for me outside the shop, but he never came in." A note of impatience, tinged with anger, crept into her voice. "Is that all you want to know?"

"May I point out, Madame Martin, that you are the one who came to get me?"

"Only because a crazy old maid practically dragged me there so she could get a close-up look at you."

"You don't like Mademoiselle Doncoeur?"

"I don't like people who can't mind their own business."

"People like Mademoiselle Doncoeur?"

"You know that we've taken in my brother-in-law's child. Believe me or not, I've done everything I can for her. I treat her the way I'd treat my own child. . . ." She paused to light a fresh cigarette, and Maigret tried unsuccessfully to picture her as a doting mother. ". . . And now that old maid is always over here, offering to help me with the child. Every time I start to go out, I find her in the hallway, smiling sweetly, and saying, 'You mustn't leave Colette all alone, Madame Martin. Let me go in and keep her company.' I sometimes wonder if she doesn't go through my drawers when I'm out."

"You put up with her, nevertheless."

"How can I help it? Colette asks for her, especially since she's been in bed. And my husband is fond of her, because when he was a bachelor, she took care of him when he was sick with pleurisy."

"Have you already returned the doll you bought for Colette's Christmas?"

She frowned and glanced at the door to the child's bedroom. "I see you've been questioning the little girl. No, I haven't taken it back for the very good reason that all the big department stores are closed today. Would you like to see it?"

She spoke defiantly, expecting him to refuse, but he said nothing. He examined the cardboard box, noting the price tag. It was a very cheap doll.

"May I ask where you went this morning?"

"I did my marketing."

"Rue Amelot or Rue du Chemin Vert?"

"Both."

"If I may be indiscreet, what did you buy?"

Furious, she stormed into the kitchen, snatched up her shopping bag, and dumped it on the dining-room table. "Look for yourself!"

There were three cans of sardines, butter, potatoes, some ham, and a head of lettuce.

She fixed him with a hard, unwavering stare. She was not in the least nervous. Spiteful, rather.

"Any more questions?"

"Yes. The name of your insurance agent."

"My insurance . . ." She was obviously puzzled.

"Insurance agent. The one who came to see you."

"I'm sorry. I was at a loss for a moment because you spoke of *my* agent as though he were really handling a policy for me. So Colette told you that, too? Actually, a man did come to see me twice, trying to sell me a policy. He was one of those door-to-door salesmen, and I thought at first he was selling vacuum cleaners, not life insurance. I had a terrible time getting rid of him."

"Did he stay long?"

"Long enough for me to convince him that I had no desire to take out a policy."

"What company did he represent?"

"He told me but I've forgotten. Something with 'Mutual' in it."

"And he came back later?"

"Yes."

"What time does Colette usually go to sleep?"

"I put out her light at seven-thirty, but sometimes she talks to herself in the dark until much later."

"So the second time the insurance man called, it was later than seven-thirty?"

"Possibly." She saw the trap. "I remember now I was washing the dishes."

"And you let him in?"

"He had his foot in the door."

"Did he call on other tenants in the building?"

"I haven't the slightest idea, but I'm sure you will inquire. Must you cross-examine me like a criminal, just because a little girl imagines she saw Santa Claus? If my husband were here——"

"By the way, does your husband carry life insurance?"

"I think so. In fact, I'm sure he does."

Maigret picked up his hat from a chair and started for the door. Madame Martin seemed surprised.

"Is that all?"

"That's all. It seems your brother-in-law promised to come and see his daughter today. If he should come, I would be grateful if you let me know. And now I'd like a few words with Mademoiselle Doncoeur."

There was a convent smell about Mademoiselle Doncoeur's apartment, but there was no dog or cat in sight, no antimacassars on the chairs, no bric-a-brac on the mantelpiece.

"Have you lived in this house long, Mademoiselle Doncoeur?"

"Twenty-five years, Monsieur l'Inspecteur. I'm one of the oldest tenants. I remember when I first moved in you were already living across the street, and you wore long mustaches."

"Who lived in the next apartment before Martin moved in?"

"A public-works engineer. I don't remember his name, but I could look it up for you. He had a wife and daughter. The girl was a deaf-mute. It was very sad. They went to live somewhere in the country."

"Have you been bothered by a door-to-door insurance agent recently?"

"Not recently. There was one who came around two or three years ago."

"You don't like Madame Martin, do you?"

"Why?"

"I asked if you liked Madame Martin."

"Well, if I had a son . . ."

"Go on."

"If I had a son I don't think I would like Madame Martin for a daughter-in-law. Especially as Monsieur Martin is such a nice man, so kind."

"You think he is unhappy with his wife?"

"I wouldn't say that. I have nothing against her, really. She can't help being the kind of woman she is."

"What kind of woman is she?"

"I couldn't say, exactly. You've seen her. You're a better judge of those things than I am. In a way, she's not like a woman at all. I'll wager she never shed a tear in her life. True, she is bringing up the child properly, decently, but she never says a kind word to her. She acts exasperated when I tell Colette a fairy tale. I'm sure she's told the girl there is no Santa Claus. Luckily Colette doesn't believe her."

"The child doesn't like her either, does she?"

"Colette is always obedient. She tries to do what's expected of her. I think she's just as happy to be left alone."

"Is she alone much?"

"Not much. I'm not reproaching Madame Martin. It's hard to explain. She wants to live her own life. She's not interested in others. She doesn't even talk much about herself."

"Have you ever met her brother-in-law—Colette's father?"

"I've seen him on the landing, but I've never spoken to him. He walks with his head down, as if he were ashamed of something. He always looks as if he slept in his clothes. No, I don't think it was he last night, Monsieur Maigret. He's not the type. Unless he was terribly drunk."

On his way out Maigret looked in at the concierge's lodge, a dark cubicle where the light burned all day.

It was noon when he started back across the boulevard. Curtains stirred at the windows of the house behind him. Curtains stirred at his own window, too. Madame Maigret was watching for him so she would know when to put the chicken in the oven. He waved to her. He wanted very much to stick out his tongue and lick up a few of the tiny snowflakes that were drifting down. He could still remember their taste.

"I WONDER IF that little tyke is happy over there," sighed Madame Maigret as she got up from the table to bring the coffee from the kitchen.

She could see that he wasn't listening. He had pushed back his chair and was stuffing his pipe while staring at the purring stove. For her own satisfaction she added, "I don't see how she could be happy with that woman."

He smiled vaguely, as he always did when he hadn't heard what she said, and continued to stare at the tiny flames licking evenly at the mica windows of the salamander. There were at least ten similar stoves in the house, all purring alike in ten similar dining rooms with wine and cakes on the table, a carafe of cordial waiting on the sideboard, and all the windows pale with the same hard, gray light of a sunless day.

It was perhaps this very familiarity that had been confusing his subconscious since morning. Nine times out of ten his investigations plunged him abruptly into new surroundings, set him at grips with people of a world he barely knew, people of a social level whose habits and manners he had to study from scratch. But in this case, which was not really a case since he had no official assignment, the whole approach was unfamiliar because the background was too familiar. For the first time in his career something professional was happening in his own world, in a building that might just as well be his building.

The Martins could easily have been living on his floor instead of across the street, and it would probably have been Madame Maigret who would look after Colette when her aunt was away. There was an elderly maiden lady living just under him who was a plumper, paler replica of Mademoiselle Doncoeur. The frames of the photographs of Martin's father and mother were exactly the same as those that framed Maigret's father and mother, and the enlargements had probably been made by the same studio.

Was that what was bothering him? He seemed to lack perspective. He was unable to look at people and things from a fresh, new viewpoint.

He had detailed his morning activities during dinner—a pleasant little Christmas dinner that had left him with an overstuffed feeling—and his wife had listened while looking at the windows across the street with an air of embarrassment.

"Is the concierge sure that nobody could have come in from outside?"

"She's not so sure any more. She was entertaining friends until after midnight. And after she had gone to bed, there were considerable comings and goings, which is natural for Christmas Eve."

"Do you think something more is going to happen?"

That was a question that had been plaguing Maigret all morning. First of all, he had to consider that Madame Martin had not come to see him spontaneously, but only on the insistence of Mademoiselle Doncoeur. If she had got up earlier, if she had been the first to see the doll and hear the story of Father Christmas, wouldn't she have kept the secret and ordered the little girl to say nothing?

And later she had taken the first opportunity to go out, even though there was plenty to eat in the house for the day. And she had been so absent-minded that she had bought butter, although there was still a pound in the cooler.

Maigret got up from the table and resettled himself in his chair by the window. He picked up the phone and called the Quai des Orfèvres.

"Lucas?"

"I got what you wanted, Chief. I have a list of all prisoners released for the last four months. There aren't as many as I thought. And none of them has lived on Boulevard Richard Lenoir at any time."

That didn't matter any more now. At first Maigret had thought that a tenant across the street might have hidden money or stolen goods under the floor before he was arrested. His first thought on getting out of jail would be to recover his booty. With the little girl bedridden, however, the room was occupied day and night. Impersonating Father Christmas would not have been a bad idea to get into the room. Had this been the case, however, Madame Martin would not have been so reluctant to call in Maigret. Nor would she have been in so great a hurry to get out of the house afterward on such a flimsy pretext. So Maigret had abandoned that theory.

"You want me to check each prisoner further?"

"Never mind. Any news about Paul Martin?"

"That was easy. He's known in every station house between the Bastille and the Hôtel de Ville, and even on Boulevard Saint Michel."

"What did he do last night?"

"First he went aboard the Salvation Army barge to eat. He's a regular there one day a week and yesterday was his day. They had a special feast for Christmas Eve and he had to stand in line quite a while."

"After that?"

"About eleven o'clock he went to the Latin Quarter and opened doors for motorists in front of a night club. He must have collected enough money in tips to get himself a sinkful, because he was picked up dead drunk near Place Maubert at four in the morning. He was taken to the station house to sleep it off, and was there until eleven this morning. They'd just turned him loose when I phoned, and they promised to bring him to me when they find him again. He still had a few francs in his pocket."

"What about Bergerac?"

"Jean Martin is taking the afternoon train for Paris. He was quite upset by a phone call he got this morning."

"He got only one call?"

"Only one this morning. He got a call last night while he was eating dinner."

"You know who called him?"

"The desk clerk says it was a man's voice, asking for Monsieur Jean Martin. He sent somebody into the dining room for Martin but when Martin got to the phone, the caller had hung up. Seems it spoiled his whole evening. He went out with a bunch of traveling salesmen to some local hot spot where there were pretty girls and whatnot, but after drinking a few glasses of champagne, he couldn't talk about anything except his wife and daughter. The niece he calls his daughter, it seems. He had such a dismal evening that he went home early. Three o'clock. That's all you wanted to know, Chief?"

When Maigret didn't reply, Lucas had to satisfy his curiosity. "You still phoning from home, Chief? What's happening up your way? Somebody get killed?"

"I still can't say. Right now all I know is that the principals are a seven-year-old girl, a doll, and Father Christmas."

"Ah?"

"One more thing. Try to get me the home address of the manager of Zenith Watches, Avenue de l'Opéra. You ought to be able to raise somebody there, even on Christmas Day. Call me back."

"Soon as I have something."

Madame Maigret had just served him a glass of Alsatian plum brandy that her sister had sent them. He smacked his lips. For a moment he was tempted to forget all about the business of the doll and Father Christmas. It would be much simpler just to take his wife to the movies. . . .

"What color eyes has she?"

It took him a moment to realize that the only person in the case who interested Madame Maigret was the little girl.

"Why, I'm not quite sure. They can't be dark. She has blond hair."

"So they're blue."

"Maybe they're blue. Very light, in any case. And they are very serious."

"Because she doesn't look at things like a child. Does she laugh?"

"She hasn't much to laugh about."

"A child can always laugh if she feels herself surrounded by people she can trust, people who let her act her age. I don't like that woman."

"You prefer Mademoiselle Doncoeur?"

"She may be an old maid but I'm sure she knows more about children than that Madame Martin. I've seen *her* in the shops. Madame Martin is one of those women who watch the scales, and take their money out of their pocketbooks, coin by coin. She always looks around suspiciously, as though everybody was out to cheat her."

The telephone rang as Madame Maigret was repeating, "I don't like that woman."

It was Lucas calling, with the address of Monsieur Arthur Godefroy, general manager in France for Zenith Watches. He lived in a sumptuous villa at Saint Cloud, and Lucas had discovered that he was at home. He added:

"Paul Martin is here, Chief. When they brought him in, he started crying. He thought something had happened to his daughter. But he's all right now—except for an awful hangover. What do I do with him?"

"Anyone around who can come up here with him?"

"Torrence just came on duty. I think he could use a little fresh air. He looks as if he had a hard night too. Anything more from me, Chief?"

"Yes. Call Palais Royal station. About five years ago a man named Lorilleux disappeared without a trace. He sold jewelry and old coins in the Palais Royal arcades. Get me all the details you can on his disappearance."

Maigret smiled as he noted that his wife was sitting opposite him with her knitting. He had never before worked on a case in such domestic surroundings.

"Do I call you back?" asked Lucas.

"I don't expect to move an inch from my chair."

A moment later Maigret was talking to Monsieur Godefroy, who had a decided Swiss accent. The Zenith manager thought that something must have happened to Jean Martin, for anyone to be making inquiries about him on Christmas Day.

"Most able . . . most devoted . . . I'm bringing him into Paris to be assistant manager next year . . . Next week, that is . . . Why do you ask? Has anything—— Be still, you!" He paused to quiet the juvenile hubbub in the background. "You must excuse me. All my family is with me today and——"

"Tell me, Monsieur Godefroy, has anyone called your office these last few days to inquire about Monsieur Martin's current address?"

"Yesterday morning, as a matter of fact. I was very busy with the holiday rush, but he asked to speak to me personally. I forget what name he gave. He said he had an extremely important message for Jean Martin, so I told him how to get in touch with Martin in Bergerac."

"He asked you nothing else?"

"No. He hung up at once. Is anything wrong?"

"I hope not. Thank you very much, monsieur."

The screams of children began again in the background and Maigret said good-by.

"Were you listening?"

"I heard what you said. I didn't hear his answers."

"A man called the office yesterday morning to get Martin's address. The same man undoubtedly called Bergerac that evening to make sure Martin was still there, and therefore would not be at his Boulevard Richard Lenoir address for Christmas Eve."

"The same man who appeared last night as Father Christmas?"

"More than likely. That seems to clear Paul Martin. He would not have to make two phone calls to find out where his brother was. Madame Martin would have told him."

"You're really getting excited about this case. You're delighted that it came up, aren't you? Confess!" And while Maigret was racking his brain for excuses, she added, "It's quite natural. I'm fascinated too. How much longer do you think the child will have to keep her leg in a cast?"

"I didn't ask."

"I wonder what sort of complications she could have had?"

Maigret looked at her curiously. Unconsciously she had switched his mind onto a new track.

"That's not such a stupid remark you just made."

"What did I say?"

"After all, since she's been in bed for two months, she should be up and around soon, barring really serious complications."

"She'll probably have to walk on crutches at first."

"That's not the point. In a few days then, or a few weeks at most, she will no longer be confined to her room. She'll go for a walk with Madame Martin. And the coast will be clear for any-one to enter the apartment without dressing up like Father Christmas."

Madame Maigret's lips were moving. While listening to her husband and watching his face, she was counting stitches.

"First of all, the presence of the child forced our man to use trickery. She's been in bed for two months—two months for him to wait. Without the complications the flooring could have been taken up several weeks ago. Our man must have had urgent reasons for acting at once, without further delay."

"Monsieur Martin will return to Paris in a few days?"

"Exactly."

"What do you suppose the man found underneath the floor?"

"Did he really find anything? If not, his problem is still as press-ing as it was last night. So he will take further action."

"What action?"

"I don't know."

"Look, Maigret, isn't the child in danger? Do you think she's safe with that woman?"

"I could answer that if I knew where Madame Martin went this morning on the pretext of doing her shopping." He picked up the phone again and called Police Judiciaire.

"I'm pestering you again, Lucas. I want you to locate a taxi that picked up a passenger this morning between nine and ten somewhere near Boulevard Richard Lenoir. The fare was a woman in her early thirties, blond, slim but solidly built. She was wearing a gray suit and a beige hat. She carried a brown shopping bag. I want to know her destination. There couldn't have been so many cabs on the street at that hour."

"Is Paul Martin with you?"

"Not yet."

"He'll be there soon. About that other thing, the Lorilleux matter, the Palais Royal boys are checking their files. You'll have the data in a few minutes."

Jean Martin must be taking his train in Bergerac at this moment. Little Colette was probably taking her nap. Mademoiselle Doncoeur was doubtless sitting behind her window curtain, wondering what Maigret was up to.

People were beginning to come out now, families with their children, the children with their new toys. There were certainly queues in front of the movie houses. . . .

A taxi stopped in front of the house. Footsteps sounded in the stairway. Madame Maigret went to the door. The deep bass voice of Torrence rumbled, "You there, Chief?"

Torrence came in with an ageless man who hugged the walls and looked humbly at the floor. Maigret went to the sideboard and filled two glasses with plum brandy.

"To your health," he said.

The man looked at Maigret with surprised, anxious eyes. He raised a trembling, hesitant hand.

"To your health, Monsieur Martin. I'm sorry to make you come all the way up here, but you won't have far to go now to see your daughter."

"Nothing has happened to her?"

"No, no. When I saw her this morning she was playing with her new doll. You can go, Torrence. Lucas must need you."

Madame Maigret had gone into the bedroom with her knitting. She was sitting on the edge of the bed, counting her stitches.

"Sit down, Monsieur Martin."

The man had touched his lips to the glass and set it down. He looked at it uneasily.

"You have nothing to worry about. Just tell yourself that I know all about you."

"I wanted to visit her this morning," the man sighed. "I swore I would go to bed early so I could wish her a Merry Christmas."

"I know that, too."

"It's always the same. I swear I'll take just one drink, just enough to pick me up. . . ."

"You have only one brother, Monsieur Martin?"

"Yes, Jean. He's six years younger than I am. He and my wife and my daughter were all I had to love in this world."

"You don't love your sister-in-law?"

He shivered. He seemed both startled and embarrassed.

"I have nothing against Loraine."

"You entrusted your child to her, didn't you?"

"Well, yes, that is to say, when my wife died and I began to slip . . ."

"I understand. Is your daughter happy?"

"I think so, yes. She never complains."

"Have you ever tried to get back on your feet?"

"Every night I promise myself to turn over a new leaf, but next day I start all over again. I even went to see a doctor. I followed his advice for a few days. But when I went back, he was very busy. He said I ought to be in a special sanatorium."

He reached for his glass, then hesitated. Maigret picked up his own glass and took a swallow to encourage him.

"Did you ever meet a man in your sister-in-law's apartment?"

"No. I think she's above reproach on that score."

"Do you know where your brother first met her?"

"In a little restaurant on Rue Beaujolais where he used to eat when he was in Paris. It was near the shop where Loraine was working."

"Did they have a long engagement?"

"I can't say. Jean was on the road for two months and when he came back he told me he was getting married."

"Were you his best man?"

"Yes. Loraine has no family in Paris. She's an orphan. So her landlady acted as her witness. Is there something wrong?"

"I don't know yet. A man entered Colette's room last night dressed as Father Christmas. He gave your girl a doll, and lifted two loose boards from the floor."

"Do you think I'm in fit condition to see her?"

"You can go over in a little while. If you feel like it you can shave here. Do you think your brother would be likely to hide anything under the floor?"

"Jean? Never!"

"Even if he wanted to hide something from his wife?"

"He doesn't hide things from his wife. You don't know him. He's one of those rare humans—a scrupulously honest man. When he comes home from the road, she knows exactly how much money he has left, to the last centime."

"Is she jealous?"

Paul Martin did not reply.

"I advise you to tell me what you know. Remember that your daughter is involved in this."

"I don't think that Loraine is especially jealous. Not of women, at least. Perhaps about money. At least that's what my poor wife always said. She didn't like Loraine."

"Why not?"

"She used to say that Loraine's lips were too thin, that she was too polite, too cold, always on the defensive. My wife always thought that Loraine set her cap for Jean because he had a good job with a future and owned his own furniture."

"Loraine had no money of her own?"

"She never speaks of her family. I understand her father died when she was very young and her mother did housework somewhere in the Glacière quarter. My poor wife used to say, 'Loraine knows what she wants.'"

"Do you think she was Lorilleux's mistress?"

Paul Martin did not reply. Maigret poured him another finger of plum brandy. Martin gave him a grateful look, but he did not touch the glass. Perhaps he was thinking that his daughter might notice his breath when he crossed the street later on.

"I'll get you a cup of coffee in a moment. . . . Your wife must have had her own ideas on the subject."

"How did you know? Please note that my wife never spoke disparagingly of people. But with Loraine it was almost pathological. Whenever we were to meet my sister-in-law, I used to beg my wife not to show her antipathy. It's funny that you should bring all that up now, at this time in my life. Do you think I did wrong in letting her take Colette? I sometimes think so. But what else could I have done?"

"You didn't answer my question about Loraine's former employer."

"Oh—yes. My wife always said it was very convenient for Loraine to have married a man who was away from home so much."

"You know where she lived before her marriage?"

"In a street just off Boulevard Sébastopol, on the right as you walk from Rue de Rivoli toward the boulevard. I remember we picked her up there the day of the wedding."

"Rue Pernelle?"

"That's it. The fourth or fifth house on the left side of the street is a quiet rooming house, quite respectable. People who work in the neighborhood live there. I remember there were several little actresses from the Châtelet."

"Would you like to shave, Monsieur Martin?"

"I'm ashamed. Still, since my daughter is just across the street . . ."

"Come with me."

Maigret took him through the kitchen so he wouldn't have to meet Madame Maigret in the bedroom. He set out the necessary toilet articles, not forgetting a clothes brush.

When he returned to the dining room, Madame Maigret poked her head through the door and whispered, "What's he doing?"

"He's shaving."

Once more Maigret reached for the telephone. He was certainly giving poor Lucas a busy Christmas Day.

"Are you indispensable at the office?"

"Not if Torrence sits in for me. I've got the information you wanted."

"In just a moment. I want you to jump over to Rue Pernelle. There's a rooming house a few doors down from Boulevard Sébastopol. If the proprietor wasn't there five years ago, try to dig up someone who lived there then. I want everything you can find out on a certain Loraine——"

"Loraine who?"

"Just a minute, I didn't think of that."

Through the bathroom door he asked Martin for the maiden name of his sister-in-law. A few seconds later he was on the phone again.

"Loraine Boitel," he told Lucas. "The landlady of this rooming house was witness at her marriage to Jean Martin. Loraine Boitel was working for Lorilleux at the time. Try to find out if she was more than a secretary to him, and if he ever came to see her. And work fast. This may be urgent. What have you got on Lorilleux?"

"He was quite a fellow. At home on Rue Mazarine he was a good respectable family man. In his Palais Royal shop he not only sold old coins and souvenirs of Paris, but he had a fine collection of pornographic books and obscene pictures."

"Not unusual for the Palais Royal."

"I don't know what else went on there. There was a big divan covered with red silk rep in the back room, but the investigation was never pushed. Seems there were a lot of important names among his customers."

"What about Loraine Boitel?"

"The report barely mentions her, except that she waited all

morning for Lorilleux the day he disappeared. I was on the phone about this when Langlois of the Financial Squad came into my office. The name Lorilleux rang a bell in the back of his mind and he went to check his files. Nothing definite on him, but he'd been making frequent trips to Switzerland and back, and there was a lot of gold smuggling going on at that time. Lorilleux was stopped and searched at the frontier several times, but they never found anything on him."

"Lucas, old man, hurry over to Rue Pernelle. I'm more than ever convinced that this is urgent."

Paul Martin appeared in the doorway, his pale cheeks close-shaven.

"I don't know how to thank you. I'm very much embarrassed."

"You'll visit your daughter now, won't you? I don't know how long you usually stay, but today I don't want you to leave until I come for you."

"I can't very well stay all night, can I?"

"Stay all night if necessary. Manage the best you can."

"Is the little girl in danger?"

"I don't know, but your place today is with your daughter."

Paul Martin drank his black coffee avidly, and started for the stairway. The door had just closed after him when Madame Maigret rushed into the dining room.

"You can't let him go to see his daughter empty-handed on Christmas Day!"

"But——" Maigret was about to say that there just didn't happen to be a doll around the house, when his wife thrust a small shiny object into his hands. It was a gold thimble that had been in her sewing basket for years but was never used.

"Give him that. Little girls always like thimbles. Hurry!"

He shouted from the landing, "Monsieur Martin! Just a minute, Monsieur Martin!"

He closed the man's fingers over the thimble. "Don't tell a soul where you got this."

Before re-entering the dining room he stood for a moment on

the threshold, grumbling. Then he sighed, "I hope you've finished making me play Father Christmas."

"I'll bet she likes the thimble as well as a doll. It's something grownups use, you know."

They watched the man cross the boulevard. Before going into the house he turned to look up at Maigret's windows, as if seeking encouragement.

"Do you think he'll ever be cured?"

"I doubt it."

"If anything happens to that woman, to Madame Martin . . ."

"Well?"

"Nothing. I was thinking of the little girl. I wonder what would become of her."

Ten minutes passed. Maigret had opened his newspaper and lighted his pipe. His wife had settled down again with her knitting. She was counting stitches when he exhaled a cloud of smoke and murmured, "You haven't even seen her."

MAIGRET WAS LOOKING for an old envelope, on the back of which he had jotted down a few notes summing up the day's events. He found it in a drawer into which Madame Maigret always stuffed any papers she found lying around the house.

This was the only investigation, he mused, that he had ever conducted practically in its entirety from his favorite armchair. It was also unusual in that no dramatic stroke of luck had come to his aid. True, luck had been on his side, in that he had been able to muster all his facts by the simplest and most direct means. How many times had he deployed scores of detectives on an all-night search for some minor detail. This might have happened, for instance, if Monsieur Arthur Godefroy of Zenith had gone home to Zurich for Christmas, or if he had been out of reach of a telephone. Or if Monsieur Godefroy had been unaware of the telephone inquiry regarding the whereabouts of Jean Martin.

When Lucas arrived shortly after four o'clock, his nose red

and his face pinched with the cold, he too could report the same kind of undramatic luck.

A thick yellow fog, unusual for Paris, had settled over the city. Lights shone in all the windows, floating in the murk like ships at sea or distant beacons. Familiar details had been blotted out so completely that Maigret half expected to hear the moan of foghorns.

For some reason, perhaps because of some boyhood memory, Maigret was pleased to see the weather thicken. He was also pleased to see Lucas walk into his apartment, take off his overcoat, sit down, and stretch out his frozen hands toward the fire.

In appearance Lucas was a reduced-scale model of Maigret—a head shorter, half as broad in the shoulders, half as stern in expression although he tried hard. Without conscious imitation but with conscious admiration Lucas had copied his chief's slightest gestures, postures, and changes of expression—even to the ceremony of inhaling the fragrance of the plum brandy before touching his lips to the glass.

The landlady of the rooming house on Rue Pernelle had been killed in a subway accident two years earlier, Lucas reported. Luckily the place had been taken over by the former night watchman, who had been in trouble with the police on morals charges.

"So it was easy enough to make him talk," said Lucas, lighting a pipe much too large for him. "I was surprised that he had the money to buy the house, but he explained that he was front man for a big investor who had money in all sorts of enterprises but didn't like to have his name used."

"What kind of place is it?"

"Looks respectable. Clean enough. Office on the mezzanine. Rooms by the month, some by the week, and a few on the second floor by the hour."

"He remembers Loraine?"

"Very well. She lived there more than three years. I got the impression he didn't like her because she was tightfisted."

"Did Lorilleux come to see her?"

"On my way to Rue Pernelle I picked up a photo of Lorilleux at the Palais Royal station. The new landlord recognized him right away."

"Lorilleux went to her room often?"

"Two or three times a month. He always had baggage with him, he always arrived around one o'clock in the morning, and always left before six. I checked the timetables. There's a train from Switzerland around midnight and another at six in the morning. He must have told his wife he was taking the six o'clock train."

"Nothing else?"

"Nothing, except that Loraine was stingy with tips, and always cooked her dinner on an alcohol burner, even though the house rules said no cooking in the rooms."

"No other men?"

"No. Very respectable except for Lorilleux. The landlady was witness at her wedding."

Maigret glanced at his wife. He had insisted that she remain in the room when Lucas came. She stuck to her knitting, trying to make believe she was not there.

Torrence was out in the fog, going from garage to garage, checking the trip sheets of taxi fleets. The two men waited serenely, deep in their easy chairs, each holding a glass of plum brandy with the same pose. Maigret felt a pleasant numbness creeping over him.

His Christmas luck held out with the taxis, too. Sometimes it took days to run down a particular taxi driver, particularly when the cab in question did not belong to a fleet. Cruising drivers were the hardest to locate; they sometimes never even read the newspapers. But shortly before five o'clock Torrence called from Saint Ouen.

"I found one of the taxis," he reported.

"One? Was there more than one?"

"Looks that way. This man picked up the woman at the corner of Boulevard Richard Lenoir and Boulevard Voltaire this morning. He drove her to Rue de Maubeuge, opposite the Gare du Nord, where she paid him."

"Did she go into the railway station?"

"No. The driver says she went into a luggage shop that stays open on Sundays and holidays. After that he doesn't know."

"Where's the driver now?"

"Right here in the garage. He just checked in."

"Send him to me, will you? Right away. I don't care how he gets here as long as it's in a hurry. Now I want you to find me the cab that brought her home."

"Sure, Chief, as soon as I get myself a coffee with a stick in it. It's damned cold out here."

Maigret glanced through the window. There was a shadow against Mademoiselle Doncoeur's curtains. He turned to Lucas.

"Look in the phone book for a luggage shop across from the Gare du Nord."

Lucas took only a minute to come up with a number, which Maigret dialed.

"Hello, this is the Police Judiciaire. Shortly before ten this morning a young woman bought something in your shop, probably a suitcase. She was a blonde, wearing a gray suit and beige hat. She carried a brown shopping bag. Do you remember her?"

Perhaps trade was slack on Christmas Day. Or perhaps it was easier to remember customers who shopped on Christmas. In any case, the voice on the phone replied:

"Certainly, I waited on her myself. She said she had to leave suddenly for Cambrai because her sister was ill, and she didn't have time to go home for her bags. She wanted a cheap suitcase, and I sold her a fiber model we have on sale. She paid me and went into the bar next door. I was standing in the doorway and a little later I saw her walking toward the station, carrying the suitcase."

"Are you alone in your shop?"

"I have one clerk on duty."

"Can you leave him alone for half an hour? . . . Fine! Then jump in a taxi and come to this address. I'll pay the fare, of course."

"And the return fare? Shall I have the cab wait?"

"Have him wait, yes."

According to Maigret's notes on the back of the envelope, the first taxi driver arrived at 5:50 P.M. He was somewhat surprised, since he had been summoned by the police, to find himself in a private apartment. He recognized Maigret, however, and made no effort to disguise his curious interest in how the famous inspector lived.

"I want you to climb to the fourth floor of the house just across the street. If the concierge stops you, tell her you're going to see Madame Martin."

"Madame Martin. I got it."

"Go to the door at the end of the hall and ring the bell. If a blonde opens the door and you recognize her, make some excuse —you're on the wrong floor, anything you think of. If somebody else answers, ask to speak to Madame Martin personally."

"And then?"

"Then you come back here and tell me whether or not she is the fare you drove to Rue de Maubeuge this morning."

"I'll be right back, Inspector."

As the door closed, Maigret smiled in spite of himself.

"The first call will make her worry a little. The second, if all goes well, will make her panicky. The third, if Torrence has any luck——"

Torrence, too, was having his run of Christmas luck. The phone rang and he reported:

"I think I've found him, Chief. I dug up a driver who picked up a woman answering your description at the Gare du Nord, only he didn't take her to Boulevard Richard Lenoir. He dropped her at the corner of Boulevard Beaumarchais and the Rue du Chemin Vert."

"Send him to me."

"He's a little squiffed."

"It doesn't matter. Where are you?"

"The Barbès garage."

"Then it won't be much out of your way to stop by the Gare du Nord. Go to the checkroom. Unfortunately it won't be the same man on duty, but try to find out if a small new suitcase was checked between nine-thirty and ten this morning. It's made of fiber and shouldn't be too heavy. Get the number of the check. They won't let you take the suitcase without a warrant, so try to get the name and address of the man on duty this morning."

"What next?"

"Phone me. I'll wait for your second taxi driver. If he's been drinking, better write down my address for him, so he won't get lost."

Madame Maigret was back in the kitchen, preparing the evening meal. She hadn't dared ask whether Lucas would eat with them.

Maigret wondered if Paul Martin were still across the street with his daughter. Had Madame Martin tried to get rid of him?

The bell rang again. Two men stood at the door.

The first driver had come back from Madame Martin's and had climbed Maigret's stairs behind the luggage dealer.

"Did you recognize her?"

"Sure. She recognized me, too. She turned pale. She ran to close a door behind her, then she asked me what I wanted."

"What did you tell her?"

"That I had the wrong floor. I think maybe she wanted to buy me off, but I didn't give her a chance. But she was watching from the window when I crossed the street. She probably knows I came here."

The luggage dealer was baffled and showed it. He was a middle-aged man, completely bald and equally obsequious. When the driver had gone, Maigret explained what he wanted, and the man objected vociferously.

"One just doesn't do this sort of thing to one's customers," he repeated stubbornly. "One simply does not inform on one's customers, you know."

After a long argument he agreed to call on Madame Martin. To make sure he didn't change his mind, Maigret sent Lucas to follow him.

They returned in less than ten minutes.

"I call your attention to the fact that I have acted under your orders, that I have been compelled——"

"Did you recognize her?"

"Will I be forced to testify under oath?"

"More than likely."

"That would be very bad for my business. People who buy luggage at the last minute are very often people who dislike public mention of their comings and goings."

"You may not have to go to court. Your deposition before the examining magistrate may be sufficient."

"Very well. It was she. She's dressed differently, but I recognized her all right."

"Did she recognize you?"

"She asked immediately who had sent me."

"What did you say?"

"I . . . I don't remember. I was quite upset. I think I said I had rung the wrong bell."

"Did she offer you anything?"

"What do you mean? She didn't even offer me a chair. Luckily. It would have been most unpleasant."

Maigret smiled, somewhat incredulously. He believed that the taxi driver had actually run away from a possible bribe. He wasn't so sure about this prosperous-looking shopkeeper who obviously begrudged his loss of time.

"Thank you for your co-operation."

The luggage dealer departed hastily.

"And now for Number Three, my dear Lucas."

Madame Maigret was beginning to grow nervous. From the kitchen door she made discreet signs to her husband, beckoning him to join her. She whispered, "Are you sure the father is still across the street?"

"Why?"

"I don't know. I can't make out exactly what you're up to, but I've been thinking about the child, and I'm a little afraid. . . ."

Night had long since fallen. The families were all home again. Few windows across the street remained dark. The silhouette of Mademoiselle Doncoeur was still very much in evidence.

While waiting for the second taxi driver Maigret decided to put on his collar and tie. He shouted to Lucas:

"Pour yourself another drop. Aren't you hungry?"

"I'm full of sandwiches, Chief. Only one thing I'd like when we go out: a tall beer, right from the spigot."

The second driver arrived at six twenty. At six thirty-five he had returned from across the street, a gleam in his eye.

"She looks even better in her negligee than she does in her street clothes," he said thickly. "She made me come in and she asked who sent me. I didn't know what to say, so I told her I was a talent scout for the Folies Bergère. Was she furious! She's a fine hunk of woman, though, and I mean it. Did you get a look at her legs?"

He was in no hurry to leave. Maigret saw him ogling the bottle of plum brandy with envious eyes, and poured him a glass—to speed him on his way.

"What are you going to do next, Chief?" Lucas had rarely seen Maigret proceed with such caution, preparing each step with such care that he seemed to be mounting an attack on some desperate criminal. And yet the enemy was only a woman, a seemingly insignificant little housewife.

"You think she'll still fight back?"

"Fiercely. And what's more, in cold blood."

"What are you waiting for?"

"The phone call from Torrence."

As if on cue, the telephone rang. Torrence, of course.

"The suitcase is here all right. It feels practically empty. As you predicted, they won't give it to me without a warrant. The checkroom attendant who was on duty this morning lives in the suburbs, near La Varenne-Saint Hilaire." A snag at last? Or at least a delay? Maigret frowned. But Torrence continued. "We won't have to go out there, though. When he finishes his day's work here, he plays cornet in a *bal musette* on Rue de Lappe."

"Go get him for me."

"Shall I bring him to your place?"

Maigret hesitated, thinking of Lucas's yearning for a glass of draft beer.

"No, I'll be across the street. Madame Martin's apartment, fourth floor."

He took down his heavy overcoat. He filled his pipe.

"Coming?" he said to Lucas.

Madame Maigret ran after him to ask what time he'd be home for dinner. After a moment of hesitation he smiled.

"The usual time," was his not very reassuring answer.

"Look out for the little girl, will you?"

AT TEN O'CLOCK THAT EVENING the investigation was still blocked. It was unlikely that anyone in the whole building had gone to sleep, except Colette. She had finally dozed off, with her father sitting in the dark by her bedside.

Torrence had arrived at seven-thirty with his part-time musician and checkroom attendant, who declared:

"She's the one. I remember she didn't put the check in her handbag. She slipped it into a big brown shopping bag." And when they took him into the kitchen he added, "That's the bag. Or one exactly like it."

The Martin apartment was very warm. Everyone spoke in low tones, as if they had agreed not to awaken the child. Nobody had eaten. Nobody, apparently, was even hungry. On their way over Maigret and Lucas had each drunk two beers in a little café on Boulevard Voltaire.

After the cornettist had spoken his piece, Maigret took Torrence aside and murmured fresh instructions.

Every corner of the apartment had been searched. Even the photos of Martin's parents had been taken from their frames, to make sure the baggage check had not been secreted between picture and backing. The dishes had been taken from their shelves and piled on the kitchen table. The cooler had been emptied and examined closely. No baggage check.

Madame Martin was still wearing her pale blue negligee. She was chain-smoking cigarettes. What with the smoke from the two men's pipes a thick blue haze swirled about the lamps.

"You are of course free to say nothing and answer no questions. Your husband will arrive at eleven-seventeen. Perhaps you will be more talkative in his presence."

"He doesn't know any more than I do."

"Does he know as much?"

"There's nothing to know. I've told you everything."

She had sat back and denied everything, all along the line. She had conceded only one point. She admitted that Lorilleux had dropped in to see her two or three times at night when she lived on Rue Pernelle. But she insisted there had been nothing between them, nothing personal.

"In other words he came to talk business—at one o'clock in the morning?"

"He used to come to town by a late train, and he didn't like to walk the streets with large sums of money on him. I already told you he might have been smuggling gold, but I had nothing to do with it. You can't arrest me for his activities."

"Did he have large sums of money on him when he disappeared?"

"I don't know. He didn't always take me into his confidence."

"But he did come to see you in your room at night?"

Despite the evidence she clung to her story of the morning's marketing. She denied ever having seen the two taxi drivers, the luggage dealer, or the checkroom attendant.

"If I had really left a package at the Gare du Nord, you would have found the check, wouldn't you?"

She glanced nervously at the clock on the mantel, obviously thinking of her husband's return.

"Admit that the man who came last night found nothing under the floor because you changed the hiding place."

"I know of nothing that was hidden under the floor."

"When you learned of his visit, you decided to move the treasure to the checkroom for safekeeping."

"I haven't been near the Gare du Nord. There must be thousands of blondes in Paris who answer my description."

"I think I know where we'll find the check."

"You're so very clever."

"Sit over here at this table." Maigret produced a fountain pen and a sheet of paper. "Write your name and address."

She hesitated, then obeyed.

"Tonight every letter mailed in this neighborhood will be examined, and I'll wager we will find one addressed in your handwriting, probably to yourself."

He handed the paper to Lucas with an order to get in touch with the postal authorities. Much to his surprise the woman reacted visibly.

"You see, it's a very old trick, Little One." For the first time he called her "Little One," the way he would have done if he were questioning her in his office, Quai des Orfèvres.

They were alone now. Maigret slowly paced the floor, while she remained seated.

"In case you're interested," Maigret said slowly, "the thing that shocks me most about you is not what you have done but the cold-blooded way you have done it. You've been dangling at the end of a slender thread since early this morning, and you still haven't blinked an eye. When your husband comes home, you'll try to play the martyr. And yet you know that sooner or later we'll discover the truth."

"But I've done nothing wrong."

"Then why do you lie?"

She did not reply. She was still far from the breaking point. Her nerves were calm, but her mind was obviously racing at top speed, seeking some avenue of escape.

"I'm not saying anything more," she declared. She sat down and pulled the hem of her negligee over her bare knees.

"Suit yourself." Maigret made himself comfortable in a chair opposite her.

"Are you going to stay here all night?" she asked.

"At least until your husband gets home."

"Are you going to tell him about Monsieur Lorilleux's visits to my room?"

"If necessary."

"You're a cad! Jean knows nothing about all this. He had no part in it."

"Unfortunately he is your husband."

When Lucas came back, they were staring at each other in silence.

"Janvier is taking care of the letter, Chief. I met Torrence downstairs. He says the man is in that little bar, two doors down from your house."

She sprang up. "What man?"

Maigret didn't move a muscle. "The man who came here last night. You must have expected him to come back, since he didn't find what he was looking for. And he might be in a different frame of mind this time."

She cast a dismayed glance at the clock. The train from Bergerac was due in twenty minutes. Her husband could be home in forty. She asked, "You know who this man is?"

"I can guess. I could go down and confirm my suspicion. I'd say it is Lorilleux and I'd say he is very eager to get back his property."

"It's not his property!"

"Let's say that, rightly or wrongly, he considers it his property. He must be in desperate straits, this man. He came to see you twice without getting what he wanted. He came back a third time disguised as Father Christmas. And he'll come back again. He'll be surprised to find you have company. I'm convinced that he'll be more talkative than you. Despite the general belief, men always speak more freely than women. Do you think he is armed?"

"I don't know."

"I think he is. He is tired of waiting. I don't know what story you've been telling him, but I'm sure he's fed up with it. The gentleman has a vicious face. There's nothing quite as cruel as a weakling with his back up."

"Shut up!"

"Would you like us to go so that you can be alone with him?"

The back of Maigret's envelope contained the following note: "10:38 P.M.—she decides to talk."

It was not a very connected story at first. It came out in bits and pieces, fragments of sentences interlarded with venomous asides, supplemented by Maigret's own guesses, which she either confirmed or amended.

"What do you want to know?"

"Was it money that you left in the checkroom?"

"Bank notes. Almost a million."

"Did the money belong to Lorilleux?"

"No more to him than to me."

"To one of his customers?"

"Yes. A man named Julian Boissy."

"What became of him?"

"He died."

"How?"

"He was killed."

"By whom?"

"By Monsieur Lorilleux."

"Why?"

"Because I gave him to understand that if he could raise enough money—real money—I might run away with him."

"You were already married?"

"Yes."

"You're not in love with your husband?"

"I despise mediocrity. All my life I've been poor. All my life I've been surrounded by people who have had to scrimp and save, people who have had to sacrifice and count centimes. I've had to scrimp and sacrifice and count centimes myself." She turned savagely on Maigret, as if he had been responsible for all her troubles. "I just didn't want to be poor any more."

"Would you have gone away with Lorilleux?"

"I don't know. Perhaps for a while."

"Long enough to get your hands on his money?"

"I hate you!"

"How was Boissy murdered?"

"Monsieur Boissy was a regular customer of long standing."

"Pornographic literature?"

"He was a lascivious old goat, sure. So are all men. So is Lorilleux. So are you, probably. Boissy was a widower. He lived alone in a hotel room. He was very rich and very stingy. All rich people are stingy."

"That doesn't work both ways, does it? You, for instance, are not rich."

"I would have been rich."

"If Lorilleux had not come back. How did Boissy die?"

"The devaluation of the franc scared him out of his wits. Like everybody else at that time, he wanted gold. Monsieur Lorilleux used to shuttle gold in from Switzerland pretty regularly. And he always demanded payment in advance. One afternoon Monsieur Boissy came to the shop with a fortune in currency. I wasn't there. I had gone out on an errand."

"You planned it that way?"

"No."

"You had no idea what was going to happen?"

"No. Don't try to put words in my mouth. When I came back, Lorilleux was packing the body into a big box."

"And you blackmailed him?"

"No."

"Then why did he disappear after having given you the money?"

"I frightened him."

"You threatened to go to the police?"

"No. I merely told him that our neighbors in the Palais Royal had been looking at me suspiciously and that I thought he ought to put the money in a safe place for a while. I told him about the loose floor board in my apartment. He thought it would only be for a few days. Two days later he asked me to cross the Belgian frontier with him."

"And you refused?"

"I told him I'd been stopped and questioned by a man who looked like a police inspector. He was terrified. I gave him some of the money and promised to join him in Brussels as soon as it was safe."

"What did he do with the corpse?"

"He put the box in a taxi and drove to a little country house he owned on the banks of the Marne. I suppose he either buried it there or threw it into the river. Nobody ever missed Monsieur Boissy."

"So you sent Lorilleux to Belgium without you. How did you keep him away for five years?"

"I used to write him, general delivery. I told him the police were after him, and that he probably would read nothing about it in the papers because they were setting a trap for him. I told him the police were always coming back to question me. I even sent him to South America."

"He came back two months ago?"

"About. He was at the end of his rope."

"Didn't you send him any money?"

"Not much."

"Why not?"

She did not reply. She looked at the clock.

"Are you going to arrest me? What will be the charge? I didn't kill Boissy. I wasn't there when he was killed. I had nothing to do with disposing of his body."

"Stop worrying about yourself. You kept the money because all your life you wanted money—not to spend, but to keep, to feel secure, to feel rich and free from want."

"That's my business."

"When Lorilleux came back to ask for money, or to ask you to keep your promise and run away with him, you used Colette as a pretext. You tried to scare him into leaving the country again, didn't you?"

"He stayed in Paris, hiding." Her upper lip curled slightly. "What an idiot! He could have shouted his name from the house-tops and nobody would have noticed."

"The business of Father Christmas wasn't idiotic."

"No? The money wasn't under the floor board any longer. It was right here under his nose, in my sewing basket."

"Your husband will be here in ten or fifteen minutes. Lorilleux across the street probably knows it. He's been in touch with Bergerac by phone, and he can read a timetable. He's surely armed. Do you want to wait here for your two men?"

"Take me away! I'll slip on a dress. . . ."

"The checkroom stub?"

"General delivery, Boulevard Beaumarchais."

She did not close the bedroom door after her. Brazenly she dropped the negligee from her shoulders and sat on the edge of the bed to pull on her stockings. She selected a woolen dress from the closet, tossed toilet articles and lingerie into an overnight bag.

"Let's hurry!"

"Your husband?"

"That fool? Leave him for the birds."

"Colette?"

She shrugged.

Mademoiselle Doncoeur's door opened a crack as they passed.

Downstairs on the sidewalk she clung fearfully to the two men, peering into the fog.

"Take her to the Quai des Orfèvres, Lucas. I'm staying here."

She held back. There was no car in sight, and she was obviously frightened by the prospect of walking into the night with only Lucas to protect her. Lucas was not very big.

"Don't be afraid. Lorilleux is not in this vicinity."

"You lied to me! You—you——"

Maigret went back into the house.

THE CONFERENCE with Jean Martin lasted two hours.

When Maigret left the house at one-thirty, the two brothers were in serious conversation. There was a crack of light under Mademoiselle Doncoeur's door, but she did not open the door as he passed.

When he got home, his wife was asleep in a chair in the dining room. His place at table was still set. Madame Maigret awoke with a start.

"You're alone?" When he looked at her with amused surprise, she added, "Didn't you bring the little girl home?"

"Not tonight. She's asleep. You can go for her tomorrow morning."

"Why, then we're going to . . ."

"No, not permanently. Jean Martin may console himself with some decent girl. Or perhaps his brother will get back on his feet and find a new wife. . . ."

"In other words, she won't be ours?"

"Not in fee simple, no. Only on loan. I thought that would be better than nothing. I thought it would make you happy."

"Why, yes, of course. It will make me very happy. But . . . but . . ."

She sniffled once and fumbled for her handkerchief. When she couldn't find it, she buried her face in her apron.

Journey Backward into Time

IT WAS ONE OF THOSE rare cases that can be solved by studying diagrams and documents and by applying police methods. In fact, when Inspector Maigret left the Quai des Orfèvres he had all the facts clearly in mind—even the position of the wine barrels.

He had expected a short jaunt into the countryside. Instead he found himself making a long journey backward into time. The train that took him to Vitry aux Loges, scarcely a hundred kilometers from Paris, was a conveyance straight from the picture books of Épinal, which he had not seen since his childhood. And when he inquired about a taxi, the people at the station thought that he was joking. He would have to make the rest of the trip in the baker's cart, they said. However, he persuaded the butcher to drive over in his delivery truck.

"How often do you go down there?" the inspector asked, naming the little village to which his investigation was taking him.

"Twice a week, regularly. Thanks to you, they'll have an extra meat delivery this week."

Maigret had been born only forty kilometers away, on the banks of the Loire, yet he was surprised by the somber, tragic aspect of this sector of the Forest of Orléans. The road ran through deep woods for ten kilometers without a sign of civilization. When the truck reached a tiny village in a clearing, Maigret asked, "Is this it?"

"The next hamlet."

It wasn't raining, but the woods were damp. The trees had lost most of their foliage, and the pale, raw light of the sky bore down heavily through the bare branches. The dead leaves were rotting on the ground. An occasional shot cracked in the distance.

"Is there much hunting around here?"

"That's probably Monsieur the Duke."

In another, smaller clearing some thirty one-story houses were clustered about the steeple of a church. None of the houses could be less than a century old, and their black tile roofs gave them an inhospitable air.

"You can let me off at the house of the Potru sisters."

"I guessed that was where you'd be going. It's right across from the church."

Maigret got out. The butcher drove on a little farther and opened the back of his delivery truck. A few housewives came to look but could not make up their minds to buy. It was not their regular day for meat.

Maigret had pored so long over the diagrams sent to Paris by the original investigators that he could have entered the house with his eyes shut. As it was, the rooms were so dark that he wasn't much better off with his eyes open. As he walked into the shop at the front of the house, he seemed to be stepping into a past century.

The room was as dimly lit as a canvas by an old master. The dark brown tonality of an ancient masterpiece was diffused over the walls and furniture—a monochrome in chiaroscuro broken only by a highlight here and there, on a glass jar or a copper kettle.

The elder of the Demoiselles Potru had lived in this house since her birth sixty-five years before—her younger sister was sixty-two. Their parents had spent their lives there before them. Nothing in the shop had changed in all that time—not the counter with its old-fashioned scales and its gleaming candy jars, nor shelves of notions, nor the grocery section with its stale odors of cinnamon and chicory, nor the zinc-covered slab that served as the village bar. A barrel of kerosene stood in a corner next to a smaller barrel of cooking oil. In the rear were two long tables, polished by time, flanked by backless benches.

A door opened at the left, and a woman in her early thirties came in, carrying a baby in her arms. She looked at Maigret.

"What is it you want?"

"Never mind about me. I'm here for the investigation. I suppose you are a neighbor?"

The woman, whose apron ballooned over a rounded belly, said, "I'm Marie Lacore. My husband is the blacksmith."

"I see." Maigret had just noticed the kerosene lamp hanging from the ceiling. So the hamlet had no electricity. . . .

The second room, which Maigret entered without invitation, would have been completely dark were it not for the two logs blazing on the hearth. The flickering light revealed an immense bed on which were piled several mattresses and a puffy, red eider-down quilt. An old woman lay motionless on the bed. Her haggard rigid face was lifeless except for the sharp, questioning eyes.

"She still can't speak?" Maigret asked Marie Lacore.

The blacksmith's wife shook her head in the negative. Maigret shrugged, sat down on a straw-bottomed chair, and began taking papers from his pockets.

There was nothing sensational about the actual crime, which had taken place five days earlier. The Potru sisters, who lived alone in the hovel, were believed to have accumulated a considerable nest egg. They owned three other houses in the village and had a long-established reputation as misers.

During the night of Saturday to Sunday their neighbors remembered hearing unusual noises but had thought nothing of it
at the time. However, a farmer passing the house at dawn on
Sunday noticed that the bedroom window was wide open, looked
in, and shouted for help.

Amélie Potru, the elder sister, was lying on the floor in a
pool of blood near the window, clad only in a red-stained nightgown. The younger sister, Marguerite, was lying on the bed, her
face turned to the wall, dead, with three knife wounds in her
chest, her cheek gashed, and one eye torn half from its socket.

Amélie was still alive. She had staggered to the window to give
the alarm but, weakened from loss of blood, had fallen uncon-
scious before she could cry out. She had no less than eleven stab
wounds in her right side and shoulder, none of them serious.

The second drawer of the dresser had been pulled out and apparently ransacked. Among the linen scattered on the floor was a
brief case of mildewed leather in which the sisters must have kept
their business papers. It was empty, but lying near by were a
savings-bank passbook, deeds to property, leases, and bills for
supplies.

The Orléans authorities who made the original investigation
sent Maigret detailed diagrams and photographs of the scene as
well as a transcript of the questioning of witnesses.

Marguerite, the dead woman, had been buried two days after
the murder. Amélie had resisted all efforts to take her to a hospital,
sinking her nails into the bed sheets, fighting off neighbors who
tried to move her, and demanding—with her eyes—that she be
left at home. She had lost all power of speech.

The medical examiner from Orléans declared that no vital organ
had been injured and that her loss of voice must be due to shock.
In any case, no sound had passed her lips for five days; yet despite
her bandages and her immobility she followed all proceedings
with her eyes. Even now her gaze never left Maigret for a moment.

Three hours after the Orléans authorities finished their investigation, they arrested a man who from the evidence must be the murderer: Marcel, illegitimate son of the dead Potru sister. The late Marguerite had given birth to Marcel when she was twenty-three, so he must be thirty-nine years old. For a while Marcel had worked with the hounds of the Duke's hunt. More recently he had been a woodcutter in the forest and lived in an abandoned tumble-down farmhouse near the Loup Pendu pond, ten kilometers from the village.

The villagers looked upon Marcel as a brute, a miserable wretch who was little better than an animal. Several times he had disappeared, leaving his wife and five children for weeks on end. He beat his family more often than he fed them. What's more, he was a drunkard.

Maigret decided to reread at the scene of the crime the transcript of Marcel's testimony: "I came on my bicycle around seven o'clock just when the old women were sitting down to eat. I had a drink at the bar, then I went out to the courtyard and killed a rabbit. I skinned it and cleaned it and my mother cooked it. My aunt yelled her head off because I ate their rabbit, but she always yells. She can't stand me . . ."

According to the testimony of other villagers, Marcel frequently came to the Potru sisters for a private spree. His mother never refused him anything, and his aunt, who was afraid of him, did nothing more than complain.

Maigret had stopped off in Orléans to see Marcel in his cell, and got further details.

"There was more argument," Marcel said, "when I took a cheese out of the shop and cut myself a hunk. Seems I shouldn't have cut into a whole cheese . . ."

"What wine were you drinking?" Maigret asked.

"Some of the wine from the shop."

"How was the room lighted?"

"The oil lamp. Well, after dinner my mother wasn't feeling well, so she went to bed. She asked me to get her some papers out of the second drawer in the dresser. She gave me the key. I took the papers over to the bed and we went over the bills. It was the end of the month."

"You took the papers out of the brief case? What else was in there?"

"Bonds. A big bundle of bonds. A hundred francs' worth. Maybe more."

"Did you go into the storeroom?"

"No."

"You didn't light a candle to go into the storeroom?"

"Never . . . At half-past nine I put the papers back in the drawer and then I left. I drank another slug of rotgut as I went out through the shop. . . . And anybody says I killed the old lady is a liar. Why don't you talk to the Yugo?"

To the great astonishment of Marcel's lawyer Maigret broke off his questioning.

Yarko, whom everyone called "The Yugo" because he was from Yugoslavia, was a bit of jetsam who had been washed into the village by the war and who had stayed on. He lived alone in the wing of a house near the Potru sisters and worked as a carter, hauling logs from the woods. He, too, was a confirmed drunkard, although for some time the Potru sisters had refused to serve him; he had run up too long a tab. One night they had asked Marcel to throw him out, and he had given the Yugo a bloody nose in the process.

The Potru sisters had another grievance against the Yugo. He kept his horses in a stable he had rented from them, a dilapidated outbuilding back of their courtyard, but he was always months behind in his rent. At this moment he was probably in the woods with his team.

Maigret continued to match his thoughts with the actual scene of the crime. Papers in hand, he walked to the fireplace where the Orléans men had found a kitchen knife among the ashes on the morning after the murder. The wooden handle had been completely burned, obviously to destroy fingerprints.

On the other hand, there had been plenty of fingerprints on

the dresser drawer and on the brief case—and all of them had been Marcel's.

On a candlestick that stood on a table in the bedroom they had found Amélie Potru's fingerprints—and only hers. Amélie's cold eyes still followed Maigret's every move.

"I suppose your mind is still made up not to speak?" he growled as he lit his pipe.

Silence.

Maigret stooped to make a chalk mark on the floor around some bloodstains that had been indicated on the diagram.

Marie Lacore asked him, "Will you be here for a few minutes? I'd like to put my dinner on the stove."

So Maigret found himself alone with the old woman in the house he already knew by heart, although he had never seen it before. He had spent a whole day and night studying the dossier with its diagrams and sketches, and Orléans had done such a thorough job of groundwork that he was not in the least surprised, except perhaps to find the sordid reality even more shocking than he had imagined.

And yet he himself was the son of peasants. He knew that such things existed—that there were still hamlets in France where people went on living as they had lived since the thirteenth and fourteenth centuries. But to be suddenly plunged into this village in the forest, into this ancient house, into the room alone with the old woman whose alert mind seemed to be stalking Maigret— all this was like entering one of those wretched hospitals where the worst of human monstrosities are hidden away from the eyes of normal men.

When he had begun to work on the case in Paris, Maigret had jotted down a few notes on the original report:

1. Why would Marcel have burned the knife handle without worrying about his fingerprints on the dresser and the brief case?

2. If he had used the candle, why had he carried it back into the bedroom and put it out?

3. Why didn't the bloodstains on the floor follow a straight line from the bed to the window?

4. Since Marcel might well have been recognized in the street at nine-thirty in the evening, why had he left the house by the front door, instead of going through the courtyard, which led directly into open country?

But there was one bit of evidence that worried even Marcel's lawyer. One of Marcel's buttons had been found in the old women's bed, a distinctive button that definitely had come from Marcel's old corduroy hunting jacket.

"When I was cleaning the rabbit, I caught my jacket on something," had been Marcel's explanation, "and one of the buttons must have pulled loose."

Maigret finished rereading his notes. He stood up and looked at Amélie with a peculiar smile on his lips. She was going to be sorely vexed at not being able to follow him with her eyes, for he opened a door and disappeared into the storeroom.

The cubicle was dimly lit by a dirty skylight. Maigret's gaze traveled from the stacks of cordwood to the four wine barrels against the wall—the barrels he had come all the way from Paris to see. The first two barrels were full. One contained red wine, and the other white. He thumped the next two barrels. They were empty. On one of the empty barrels several tears of tallow had fallen and congealed. Technicians from Identité Judiciaire reported that the tallow on the barrel was identical with the tallow of the candle in the bedroom.

The report of the inspector in charge from Orléans had this to say about the evidence:

"The candle drippings on the barrel were probably left by Marcel when he came to drink wine. His wife admits that he was quite drunk when he got home that night, and the zigzag tire tracks of his bicycle confirm this fact."

Maigret looked about him for something he had expected to find but which apparently was not there. Puzzled, he stepped back into the bedroom, opened the window, and called to two urchins who were gaping at the house.

"Listen, boys. Will one of you run and get me a saw?"

"A wood saw?"

"Right."

Maigret could still feel the old woman's eyes boring into his back—live eyes in a dead face, eyes that moved only when his bulky figure moved.

The boys came back bringing two saws of different sizes. At the same time Marie Lacore returned from next door.

"I hope I haven't kept you waiting," she said. "I left the baby home. Now I'll have to attend to——"

"Wait just a few minutes, will you?" That was a scene that Maigret intended to skip, thank you! He'd had enough without it. He went back into the storeroom and started sawing one of the empty barrels—the one with the candle drippings on it.

He knew what he would find. He was sure of his theory. If he had had any lingering doubts about it when he arrived, they had been dispelled by the atmosphere of the old house. Amélie Potru had turned out to be exactly the sort of person he had anticipated. And the very walls of the house seemed to ooze the avarice and hate he had expected.

Another thing. When he first entered the shop, Maigret had noted a pile of newspapers on the counter. That was one important fact the Orléans reports had omitted—that the Potru sisters were also the news dealers of the village. Further, Amélie owned glasses that, since she did not wear them about the house, were obviously reading glasses. So Amélie was able to read—and thus the biggest question mark in Inspector Maigret's theory was eliminated. His theory was based on hate—a festering hate made even more purulent by long years of being shut up together within the same four walls, of sharing the same narrow interests by day, and even the same bed by night.

But there was one experience the two sisters had not shared. Marguerite, the younger, had had a child. She had known love and motherhood. Amélie had shared only the annoying aftermath. The brat had clung to her skirts, too, for ten or fifteen years. And after he had struck out for himself, he was always coming back to eat and drink and to demand money.

It was Amélie's money as much as it was Marguerite's. More, really, since Amélie was the elder and therefore had been working and earning longer.

So Amélie hated Marcel with a hate nourished by a thousand incidents of their daily life—the rabbit he had killed, the cheese he had brazenly cut into, thus spoiling its sale value. And his mother had not said a word in protest—she never did.

Yes, Amélie read the newspapers. She must have read about the scandals, the crimes, the murder trials that take up so much space in certain papers. If so, she would know the importance of fingerprints. Then, too, Amélie was afraid of her nephew. She must have been furious with her sister for showing him the hiding place of their treasure, for letting him touch the bonds he most certainly coveted.

"One of these days he'll come to murder us both."

Surely those words had been uttered in the house dozens of times, Maigret reflected as he sawed away at the wine barrel. He realized that he was perspiring and stopped sawing long enough to take off his hat and coat. He placed them on the next barrel.

The rabbit . . . the cheese . . . then suddenly the remembrance that Marcel had left his prints on the dresser drawer and the brief case. And if that was not enough, there was the readily identifiable button, which his mother, having already gone to bed, had not yet sewed back on his jacket.

If Marcel had killed for gain, why had he emptied the brief case on the floor instead of taking it with him, bonds and all? As for Yarko the Yugoslav, Maigret had learned that he could not read.

Maigret's reasoning had begun with Amélie's wounds—eleven of them. There were too many by far and all of them were too superficial not to be extremely suspicious. Besides, they were all on the right side. She must have been clumsy, as well as afraid of pain. She wanted neither to die nor to suffer. She had expected help from the neighbors after she had opened the window to scream . . .

Would a murderer have given her time to run to the window?

And fate had laughed at her too. She had lost consciousness before her cries had awakened anyone, so she had spent the night on the floor, with nobody to stanch her bleeding.

Yes, that must have been the way it happened. It could not have been otherwise. She had killed her drowsing sister; then, her fingers wrapped in cloth of some kind to prevent leaving prints, she had opened the drawer and rifled the brief case. The bonds must disappear if Marcel were to be suspected!

Hence the candle . . .

Afterward she had sat on the edge of the bed, gashing herself timidly and awkwardly, then had gone to the fireplace (the bloodstains marked her course) to throw the knife into the embers. Finally she had walked to the window and . . .

Maigret stopped sawing. From the other room came the sound of voices raised in argument. He turned abruptly, watched the door opening slowly. The fantastic yet sinister figure of Amélie Potru stood on the threshold, swathed in bandages, wearing a curious petticoat and camisole. She stared hard at Maigret while behind her Marie Lacore protested shrilly that she had no business getting out of bed.

Maigret did not have the heart to speak to her. He finished sawing open the barrel in silence. He did not even sigh contentedly when he saw the government securities and railway bonds, still curling slightly from having been rolled up and pushed through the bung.

Had he followed his inclination, he would have beat a hasty retreat, first taking a long swig of rum straight from the bottle, the way Marcel would have done.

Amélie still spoke not a word. She stood silent, her mouth partly open. If she fainted, she would fall back into the arms of

Marie Lacore, who, in her advanced state of pregnancy, might not be able to catch her.

Well, what of it? This was a scene from another world, another age. Maigret picked up the bonds and walked toward Amélie. She backed away from him.

He dropped the securities on the bedroom table and said to Marie Lacore, "Go get the mayor. I want him as a witness."

His voice rasped a little because his vocal cords were strangely tight. Then he nodded to Amélie: "You'd better get back to bed."

Despite his case-hardened professional curiosity he turned his back to her. He knew that she had obeyed him, for he heard the bedsprings creak. He stood looking out the window until the farmer who served as mayor of the hamlet made a timid, apologetic entrance.

There was no telephone in the village. A man on a bicycle carried the message to Vitry aux Loges. The gendarmes arrived at almost the same moment the butcher's delivery truck came rolling out of the woods.

The sky shone with the same pale, raw light. The trees stirred uneasily in the west wind.

"Find anything?" asked the brigadier from the gendarmerie.

Maigret's reply was evasive. He spoke haltingly, without elation, although he knew that the case of the Potru sisters would be the subject of long commentary and review by the criminologists not only of Paris but of London, Berlin, Vienna, even New York.

Listening to him now, the brigadier might well have suspected that Inspector Maigret was drunk—or, at least, a little tipsy.

Stan the Killer

MAIGRET PUFFED AT HIS PIPE as he walked along slowly, hands clasped behind his back. It was not a simple matter to push his heavy body through the morning mob on Rue Saint Antoine, where a bright sun poured down on carts and baskets of fruits and vegetables, blocking almost the entire width of the sidewalk.

It was marketing time—the time for feeling artichokes and tasting cherries, the time for scallops and chops to take turns in the scales.

"Fine asparagus, five francs a bundle!"

"Get your fresh whiting, just come in!"

Clerks in white aprons, butchers in fine checks; the smell of cheese from a dairy shop and farther off a whiff of roasting coffee; the ping of cash registers and the rumble of a bus; the distrustful glances of housewives—all the agitated business of alimentation . . . and in the midst of it the slow heavy progress of Maigret, on one of his most tormenting cases.

Across from Rue de Birague there's a little café, with a scant three tables in front of it, called the Barrel of Burgundy. There Maigret settled himself, like any other weary passer-by. He did not even look up at the tall thin waiter who came for his order. "Small white Mâcon," he muttered—and who was to guess that this occasionally inept new waiter at the Barrel of Burgundy was otherwise known as Detective Janvier?

The waiter returned with the wine precariously balanced on a tray. He wiped the table with a questionable cloth, and was even so clumsy as to drop a scrap of paper on the floor. Maigret picked it up as he left, and read:

> *The woman's gone out marketing. No sign of One-Eye. The Beard left early. The three others must be still in the hotel.*

At ten in the morning the crowd was getting even worse. Next to the Barrel a grocery was having a sale and barkers kept entreating the passers-by to sample cookies at two francs a box.

At the corner of Rue de Birague you could see the sign of a dingy hotel, "Rooms by the month, the week or the day. Payment in advance." With doubtless intentional irony this rattrap had chosen to call itself the Beauséjour.

Maigret sipped at his light dry white wine and stared apparently aimlessly at the teeming crowd in the spring sun. But his gaze soon settled on a window in the second floor of a house on Rue de Birague opposite the hotel. At that window a little old man sat by a canary's cage and seemed to have no interest in life but to bask in the sun as long as the Lord should deign to leave him alive.

And this old gentleman, who took no notice of Maigret, was Sergeant Lucas, deftly aged some twenty years.

All this constituted a state of siege that is more vulgarly known to the police as a stake-out. It had lasted six days, and at least twice a day the inspector came around for the latest news. At night his men were relieved by a patrolman who was actually a detective from the Police Judiciaire, and a streetwalker who contrived to walk the streets without ever picking up a customer.

Maigret would have Lucas's report in a moment, by telephone; it would undoubtedly prove to be no more sensational than Janvier's.

The crowd shoved by so close to the tiny terrace of the Barrel of Burgundy that Maigret found himself constantly obliged to pull his legs back under his chair. And now, as he made one of these shifts, he suddenly realized that a man had sat down unnoticed at the same table. He was a little man, with red hair and sad eyes, whose mournful face had something of the clown about it.

"You again?" the inspector grunted.

"I beg you to forgive me, Monsieur Maigrette, but I am certain that you will eventually come to understand me and to accept the proposition that I——" He broke off to say to the waiterly Janvier, "The same as my friend."

He had an extremely marked Polish accent. He presumably suffered from throat trouble; he constantly chewed at a "cigar" impregnated with creosote, which emphasized the clownishness of his appearance.

"You're getting on my nerves!" Maigret burst out. "Will you kindly tell me how you knew I'd come here this morning?"

"I did not know."

"Then why are you here? Are you going to try to convince me that this is an accidental meeting?"

"No."

The little man's reflexes were as leisurely as those of the slow-motion acrobats in vaudeville. His yellow eyes gazed around him, staring into emptiness. He spoke in a sad voice, unvarying in pitch, as though perpetually offering condolences.

"You are not nice to me, Monsieur Maigrette."

"That isn't answering my question. How do you happen to be here this morning?"

"I followed you."

"From Headquarters?"

"Long before that. From your home."

"So you admit you're spying on me?"

"I am not spying on you, Monsieur Maigrette. I have far too much respect and admiration for you! I have already stated to you that I shall one day be your collaborator. . . ."

And he sighed nostalgically, contemplating the artificial ash of painted wood that tipped his creosote cigar.

THERE'D BEEN NOTHING about it in any of the papers save one; and that one, which got the tip the Lord knows where, uniquely complicated the Inspector's task.

> *The police have reason to believe that the Polish bandits, including Stan the Killer, are at this moment in Paris.*

It was true enough, but silence would have been more helpful.

In four years a gang of unknown Poles had attacked five farms, always in the North of France, always with the same methods.

In each case it was an isolated farm run by elderly people. The crime invariably took place the night of a market day, and the chosen victims were always those who had sold a good number of fowls and animals and had a large sum of cash on hand.

Nothing scientific about the procedure. Brutal attack, as in the days of the highway robbers. Absolute contempt for human life. These Poles were killers. They killed every human being they found on the farm, even down to the children; it was the one way of making sure that they could never be identified.

Were there two of them? Or five or eight?

In every case neighbors had noticed a small truck. One twelve-year-old claimed that he had seen a one-eyed man. Some asserted that the bandits wore black masks.

Whatever the facts, one thing was certain: Every inhabitant of each farm had had his throat sliced.

This was no business of the Paris police. This was up to the mobile units in the provinces, who worked on it for two years without remotely clarifying the mystery—a failure that did not reassure the countryside.

Then a report came in from Lille, where whole villages are Polish enclaves in French territory. The report was vague enough; it was impossible even to establish its ultimate source.

"The Poles say that this is Stan the Killer's gang. . . ."

But when the police tried to question the coal miners one by one, the men had never heard of it, or muttered, "Well, they told me . . ."

"Who's 'they'?"

"I don't know. I forget . . ."

Then came the crime near Rheims. There the gang overlooked a servant girl sleeping in the attic, who became the first survivor. She had heard the murderers talking in a language she thought was Polish. She had seen their masks through a hole in the boards; and had noticed that one of the men had only one eye and that another, a giant of a man, was extraordinarily hairy.

And so the police had come to refer to them as "Stan the Killer," "The Beard," and "One-Eye."

For months nothing more turned up, until a detective on the hotel squad made a discovery. His territory was the Saint Antoine district, which teems with Poles. And in a hotel on Rue de Birague he observed a suspicious group that included a one-eyed man and a giant whose face was literally covered with hair.

They were seemingly poor people. The bearded giant and his wife rented a room by the week, but almost every night they gave shelter to several compatriots, sometimes two, sometimes as many as five, and often other Poles rented the adjoining room.

"You want to take this over, Maigret?" the director of the Police Judiciaire suggested.

Everything was strictly hush-hush—and so the next day one

newspaper printed the story. The day after that Maigret found a letter in his mail—clumsily written in an almost childish hand, full of misspellings, on the cheap sort of paper sold in grocery stores:

> *You won't ever get Stan. Look out. Before you can*
> *take him, he'll have time to kill off plenty more.*

The letter was no hoax, Maigret was certain; it *felt* right. It had the filthy aftertaste of the underworld.

"Be careful," the chief recommended. "Don't rush into an arrest. The man who's cut sixteen throats in four years won't hesitate to scatter a few bullets around him when he sees he's done for."

Which was why Janvier had become a waiter and Lucas a basking old man.

The noisy life of the quarter went on with no suspicion that a desperate man might at any moment start firing in all directions. . . .

And then Michael Ozep appeared.

His first meeting with Maigret had been four days ago. He had arrived at Headquarters and insisted on seeing the inspector personally. Maigret had let him wait a good two hours, but the little man was undaunted. He entered the office, clicked his heels, bowed, and extended his hand:

"Michael Ozep, former officer in the Polish Army, now professor of gymnastics in Paris——"

"Sit down. I'm listening."

The Pole spoke so volubly and with so pronounced an accent that it was sometimes impossible to follow him. He explained that he came of very good family, that he had been forced to leave Poland because of unmentionably intimate misfortunes (he allowed his listener to gather that he had been in love with his colonel's wife), and that he had now sunk to worse depths of despair than ever because he could not accustom himself to leading a mediocre life.

"You understand, Monsieur Maigrette . . ." (it was impossible to wean him from that pronunciation) ". . . I am a gentleman. Here I am forced to give lessons to individuals of no culture and no education. I am a poor man . . . I have decided to commit suicide."

"A nut . . ." Maigret thought to himself. An astonishing number of the unbalanced feel the need of confiding their problems to the police; he was used to such visits.

"I tried it three weeks ago. I threw myself into the Seine from the Austerlitz Bridge, but the river squad saw me and pulled me out."

Maigret invented a pretext to step into the next office and phone the river squad. The story was true.

"Six days later I tried to kill myself with gas, but the postman came with a letter and opened the door. . . ."

A phone call to the police station in Ozep's district. And again the story was true.

"I truly *want* to kill myself, do you understand? My existence has lost all value. A gentleman cannot consent to live in poverty and mediocrity. Therefore I thought that you might have need of a man like me . . ."

"For what?"

"To help you to arrest Stan the Killer."

Maigret frowned. "You know him?"

"No. I have only heard talk about him. As a Pole, I am indignant that a man of my people should so violate the laws of hospitality. I should like to see Stan and his gang arrested. I know that he is resolved to sell his life dearly. Among those who go to arrest him, some will certainly be killed. Is it not better then that it should be I, since I already desire to die? Tell me where Stan is. I shall go and disarm him. If need be, I shall wound him so that he can do no more harm."

All Maigret found himself capable of saying was the traditional formula, "Leave your address. I'll write you a letter."

Michael Ozep had a furnished room on Rue des Tournelles, not far from Rue de Birague. The report of the investigating detective was in his favor. He had indeed been a second lieutenant in the Polish Army when it was organized after Poland gained her independence. Then his trail vanished. In Paris he tried to teach gymnastics to the sons and daughters of small merchants. His suicide attempts were genuine.

Nevertheless Maigret sent him, with the chief's approval, an official letter ending:

> . . . *deeply regret that I cannot take advantage of your generous proposition, for which my most sincere thanks* . . .

Twice since then Ozep had appeared at the Quai des Orfèvres and insisted on seeing the inspector. The second time he had even refused to leave, claiming that he could wait as long as he was obliged to, and thus almost forcibly occupying, hour after hour, one of the green plush armchairs in the waiting room.

And now Ozep sat there, at Maigret's table, in front of the Barrel of Burgundy.

"I wish to prove to you, Monsieur Maigrette, that I am of some use and that you can accept my services. It is now three days that I have been following you, and I am in a position to tell you everything that you have done during that time. I know too that the waiter who just brought my wine is one of your detectives and that there is another at the window across from us, near a canary cage."

Maigret clenched the bit of his pipe furiously between his teeth and kept his eyes turned away from the Pole, who kept on and on in his monotonous voice:

"I understand that when a strange man comes to you and says, 'I am a former officer of the Polish Army and I wish to kill myself'—I understand why you would think, 'This may not be true.' But you have verified everything that I have told you. You have seen that I do not stoop to lies. . . ."

He was a mill grinding out words, rapidly, jerkily. It wore Maigret out merely to listen to him, especially since the accent so distorted each syllable that Maigret had to concentrate to follow the sense.

"You are not a Pole, Monsieur Maigrette. You do not speak the language; you do not comprehend the mentality. I earnestly desire to help you; for I cannot see the good name of my native land tarnished by . . ."

The inspector was beginning to choke with anger. The former second lieutenant could hardly fail to observe the fact, but he continued nevertheless:

"If you try to capture Stan, what will he do? He has maybe two, maybe three, revolvers in his pockets. He fires at everybody. Who knows how many ladies he wounds? How many little babies he kills? Then people will say that the police——"

"Will you shut up?"

"Now as for me, I am resolved to die. No one will weep for poor Ozep. You say to me, 'There is Stan!' And I follow him as I have followed you. I wait for the moment when there is no one near us and I say, 'You are Stan the Killer!' Then he fires at me and I shoot him in the leg. By the fact that he shoots me, you have your proof that he is Stan and you are not making a blunder. And since he is crippled by my shot . . ."

There was no stopping him. He would have gone on in spite of the entire universe.

"Supposing I have you arrested?" Maigret broke in crudely.

"Why?"

"To get a little peace!"

"What would you say? What has poor Ozep done in violation of the laws of France, which he wishes only to defend and for which he is offering up his life?"

"Stuff it!"

"I beg your pardon? Are you agreeing?"

"Not in the least."

At that moment a woman went by, a woman with blond hair and clear complexion, recognizably a foreigner. She was carrying a shopping bag and was headed for a butcher shop.

Maigret was following her with his eyes when he noticed that his companion had suddenly set to mopping his brow with an enormous handkerchief that all but swallowed up his small-featured face.

"That is the mistress of Stan, is it not?" Ozep asked.

"Will you leave me alone?"

"You have convinced yourself that this is the mistress of Stan, but you do not know which one is Stan. You think it is the one with the beard. Now the bearded one is called Boris. And the man with one eye is Sasha. He is not a Pole, but a Russian. If you should investigate them yourself you will learn nothing. In the hotel there are only Poles; they will refuse to answer or they will lie to you. Whereas I . . ."

No housewife shopping in the confusion of Rue Saint Antoine could suspect the subjects being discussed on the tiny terrace of the Barrel of Burgundy. The blond foreigner was buying chops at a nearby butcher's stall; in her eyes there was something of that same lassitude that lay in the eyes of Michael Ozep.

"Perhaps you are angry with me because you fear that you may be called to account if I am killed? In the first place, I have no family. In the second place, I have written a letter in which I state that I alone, and purely of my own volition, have sought this death. . . ."

Poor Janvier stood on the threshold trying to figure out a way of telling Maigret that there was a telephone message for him. Maigret noticed the ambiguous pantomime, but went on watching the Pole and puffing forth little clouds of pipe smoke.

"Listen, Ozep."

"Yes, Monsieur Maigrette?"

"If you're seen again anywhere around Rue Saint Antoine, I'll have you arrested!"

"But I live only——"

"You'd better move."

"You are refusing this offer which I——"

"Get out!"

"But——"

"Get out, or I'll arrest you here and now!"

The little man rose, clicked his heels, bowed almost double, and executed a dignified retreat. Maigret had noticed one of his detectives near by; now he signaled the man to follow the peculiar professor of gymnastics.

At last Janvier could deliver his message. "Lucas just phoned. He's spotted that they have guns in the room. Five Poles slept in the next room last night, leaving the door open between. Some of them had to sleep on the floor. Who the devil was that character you were talking to?"

"Nothing . . . How much?"

Janvier slipped back into character, pointing at Ozep's glass. "You're paying Monsieur's check? One franc twenty and one twenty makes two forty."

Maigret took a taxi to Headquarters. At the door of his office he found the detective who had set out after Ozep.

"You lost him?" he roared. "Aren't you ashamed of yourself? I give you the most childish job of shadowing and you——"

"I didn't lose him," the detective murmured humbly.

"Where is he?"

"Here."

"You pulled him in?"

"He pulled me."

For Ozep had, indeed, headed directly for Headquarters, where he had placidly installed himself and his sandwich in the waiting room, after announcing that he had an appointment with Inspector "Maigrette."

THERE'RE NO KUDOS in paper work, but there may be the solution of a case.

Unwillingly, irritatedly, Maigret was adding up in one report in his own large handwriting the various information obtained in the two weeks' siege of the Polish gang.

When he set down the facts in order, he could see even more easily how very little they had learned. They did not even know precisely how many individuals belonged to the gang. The earlier reports, from the people who had seen or thought they had seen the bandits near the time of the attacks, stated that there were four of them, sometimes five. It was probable that they had other accomplices, who cased the farms and markets beforehand. That brought the number to six or seven, which seemed to correspond roughly with the number who hung around the nucleus on Rue de Birague.

There were only three regular tenants, all of whom had filled out their cards according to regulations and displayed passports in perfect order:

1. Boris Saft, the one the police called The Beard, who seemed to live as man and wife with the pale blonde.

2. Olga Tzerewski, 28, born in Vilna.

3. Sasha Vorontsov, known as One-Eye.

Boris the Beard and Olga occupied one room, Sasha One-Eye the next; the door between was always left open.

The young woman did the shopping every morning and cooked the meals on an alcohol stove.

The Beard rarely went out, but spent most of his days stretched on the iron bedstead, reading Polish newspapers that he had one of the gang buy for him at the newspaper kiosk in Place de la Bastille. Once the errand boy brought back an American detective magazine in addition to the Polish periodicals. They all read that.

One-Eye went out often, always followed by one of Maigret's detectives. A fact of which he was probably aware, since he never did more than take long walks through Paris, stopping in many bars but never speaking to a soul.

As for the rest, they were what Lucas called "the floating population." People came and went, always the same lot, four or five of them. Olga fed them, and sometimes they slept on the floor overnight. There was nothing odd about this; it happens in all hotels with poor tenants—exiles who get together to rent a room and then put up any of their compatriots they come across.

On the floating population Maigret had a few notes:

1. The Chemist, so called because he had twice visited the Work Exchange to apply for a job in a chemical plant. His clothes were badly worn but rather well cut. For hours he would wander around the streets of Paris like a man looking for any way to earn a little money; and once, for a whole day, he was employed as a sandwich man.

2. Spinach, named after the implausible spinach-green hat that seemed even more unlikely in view of his faded pink shirt. Spinach went out particularly in the evenings, when he picked up tips opening car doors in front of the Montmartre bars.

3. Puffy, a fat, wheezy little man, better dressed than the others even if his shoes were not mates.

And there were two others who visited the hotel less regularly; it was hard to say if they belonged to the gang.

Maigret stared at the notes with the exasperated feeling that the most important detail was somehow eluding him. Finally he picked up his pen again and wrote: "These people give the impression of penniless foreigners, looking for any kind of work at all. But there's always vodka in the rooms, and sometimes impressive spreads of food. Maybe the gang knows it's being watched, and is putting on an act for the police. If one of them is Stan the Killer, it is probably either The Beard or One-Eye. But this is only guesswork."

It was without the least enthusiasm that he brought his report to the chief.

"Nothing new?"

"Nothing specific. I'd swear the devils have spotted one of our men and are just amusing themselves seeing how often they can come in and go out on innocent errands. They know we can't keep a large section of the force mobilized on their account forever. Time's on their side; they have lots of it. . . ."

"You have a plan?"

"Look, Chief. You know that ideas and I haven't been on speaking terms for a long time. I come and I go and I sniff around. You'll hear people say I'm waiting for inspiration; they're way off the track. What I'm waiting for is the one significant happening that never fails to turn up. The whole thing is being there when it does turn up so that I can take advantage of it."

"So you're waiting for a . . . happening?" the chief smiled. He knew his man.

"This much I'm convinced of: This *is* the Polish gang. Because of that fool of an informer who keeps hanging around here picking up scraps of conversation, they're on their guard. Now what I want to know is, why did Stan write to me? Maybe because he knows the police always hesitate to make a forcible arrest. More probably out of sheer bravado. These killers have their pride—you might almost say, professional pride. But which of them is Stan? And why that nickname? It's more American than Polish.

"You know how I take my time before I reach any conclusions. Well, it's beginning to come . . . The last two or three days I've begun to get the feel of the psychology of these boys. Very different from French murderers.

"They need money, not to retire to the country, or to have a fling in the night spots, or to clear out to foreign parts—but just simply to live their own lives, which to them means doing nothing—eating, drinking, sleeping, spending your days stretched out on a bed, smoking cigarettes, and killing bottles of vodka. And they have this longing to be together—to dream together, gossip together, some nights sing together.

"The way I see it, after their first crime they lived like this until the money ran out; then they got ready for another job. Whenever the funds are low, they start in again, coldly, without remorse, without a trace of pity for the old people whose throats they cut—and whose life's savings they eat up in a few weeks or months . . . And now that I've got the feel of it, I'm waiting——"

"I know. For the happening . . ." the director smiled.

"Joke about it all you want. Just the same the happening may be here already."

"Where?"

"In the waiting room. The little man who calls me Maigrette and who wants at all costs to help in the arrest, even if it costs him his skin. He claims it's just another method of suicide."

"A crackpot?"

"Could be. Or an accomplice of Stan's who's using this method of keeping in touch with what we're doing. Any hypothesis fits; that's what makes my character with the creosote cigar so fascinating."

Maigret emptied his pipe by tapping it gently on the window ledge, so that the ashes fell somewhere on the Quai des Orfèvres, perhaps on the hat of a passer-by.

"He bothers me, that little man," he added. "I've seen his face somewhere. It's not in our files, but I've seen it. And I've seen the girl, too, the blonde; she's worth remembering. None of the others. Just those two."

The director of the Police Judiciaire leaned forward. "We've been going on the assumption that the blonde is Stan's mistress. You associate her and the little man. You see the possible implication?"

"That my little man is Stan himself? Could be."

"Are you going to accept this man's offer?"

"I think so." The inspector headed for the door. He felt that he'd said enough. "You'll see, Chief. I'll be amazed if we still need the stake-out by the end of this week."

And this was Thursday afternoon.

"sɪᴛ ᴅᴏᴡɴ! Doesn't it get on your nerves to suck at that filthy creosote cigar all day?"

"No, Monsieur Maigrette."

"That 'Maigrette' of yours is beginning to get me . . . But anyway, let's get down to business. Are you still set on dying?"

"Yes, Monsieur Maigrette."

"And you still want to be entrusted with a perilous mission?"

"I wish to help you to arrest Stan the Killer."

"So if I told you to go up to One-Eye and fire a bullet into his leg, you'd do it?"

"Yes, Monsieur Maigrette. But you would first have to give me a revolver. I am a poor man and——"

"Now suppose I tell you to go to The Beard or One-Eye and say that you have important information—that the police are coming to arrest them?"

"Gladly, Monsieur Maigrette. I shall wait until One-Eye passes by in the street and then I shall perform my commission."

The lowering gaze of the inspector had no effect on the little Pole. Rarely had Maigret seen a man who combined such self-assurance with such utter serenity. Michael Ozep spoke of killing himself or of visiting the Polish gang as simply, as naturally, as he might refer to brushing his teeth. He was as much at ease in police headquarters as in the Barrel of Burgundy.

"You've never met either of them?"

"No, Monsieur Maigrette."

"All right. I'm going to give you the job. And if there's any trouble, it's on your head." Maigret lowered his eyelids to conceal his too sharp interest in the other's reaction. "In a minute we'll go together to Rue Saint Antoine. I'll wait for you outside. You'll go up to the room, picking a time when the woman is there alone. You'll tell her you're a fellow Pole and you happened by chance to learn that the police are raiding the hotel tonight. . . ."

Ozep said nothing.

"You understand?"

"Yes."

"It's all set?"

"I must confess something to you, Monsieur Maigrette . . ."

"You're turning yellow?"

"Yellow? I do not under—ah! yes. No, I am not turning yellow. But I should prefer to arrange the matter in a different way. You may think that I am taking much upon myself . . . is that how I say it? But I am a timid man with the ladies. And the ladies are intelligent, far more intelligent than we men. Therefore, she will see that I am lying. And because I know that she will see that I am lying, I shall blush. And when I blush . . ."

Maigret sat motionless, absorbing this unlikely explanation.

"I should prefer to talk to a man. To the one with the beard, if you like, or the one you call One-Eye, or anyone at all. . . ."

A ray of sunlight pierced slantwise through the office and lit full on Maigret's face. He seemed to be dozing, like a man whose injudiciously heavy lunch obliges him to take a siesta at his desk.

"It is exactly the same thing, Monsieur Maigrette . . ."

But Monsieur Maigrette did not answer. The only sign that he was still alive was the slim blue spiral that rose from his pipe.

"I am desolated. You can ask of me what you wish; but you demand precisely the one thing which——"

"Stuff it!"

"I beg your pardon?"

"I say, 'Stuff it!' Which means, in French, to shut up. Where did you know the woman Olga Tzerewski?"

"I?"

"Answer me!"

"I do not understand what you mean . . ."

"Answer me!"

"I do not know this woman. If I knew her, I would tell you so. I am a former officer of the Polish Army and if I had not suffered misfortunes——"

"Where did you know her?"

"I swear to you, Monsieur Maigrette, by the head of my sainted mother and my poor father——"

"*Where did you know her?*"

"Why have you suddenly stopped being nice to me? You talk to me so brutally! To me, who came here to place myself at your disposal, to prevent Frenchmen from being murdered by a compatriot——"

"Cut the pitch!"

"Pitch?"

"Sales talk, to you. You aren't selling me."

"Ask anything of me, no matter what——"

"That's what I'm doing!"

"Ask me anything else—to throw myself under a subway train——"

"I'm asking you to go see that woman and tell her that we'll make a raid tonight."

"You insist?"

"Take it or leave it."

"And if I refuse?"

"Then you'd better see to it that I never lay eyes on you again."

"Are you really going to arrest the gang tonight?"

"Probably."

"And you will allow me to help you?"

"Possibly. We'll see about that when you've finished your first job."

"At what time?"

"Your job?"

"No. At what time will you make the raid?"

"Let's say one in the morning."

"I am going."

"Where?"

"To find the woman."

"Just a minute! We're going together."

"It is better that I go alone. If one of them sees us, he will understand that I am assisting the police. . . ."

The Pole had hardly left the office, of course, before the inspector had set a detective at his heels.

"Should I keep under cover?" the detective asked.

"No use. He's smarter than you are and he knows very well I'll have him followed."

And without losing a moment Maigret hurried downstairs and leaped into a taxi.

"Corner of Rue de Birague and Rue Saint Antoine, as fast as you can make it!"

IT WAS A RADIANT AFTERNOON. Striped awnings lent a note of color to the shops. In their shadows dogs sprawled and napped, and all life seemed to run in slow motion. You felt that even the buses had a hard time making headway in the hot heavy air. Their wheels left tracks in the heated asphalt.

Maigret sprang out of the taxi into the house on the corner. On the second floor he opened a door without bothering to knock and found Lucas sitting at the window, still in the role of a quiet and curious elderly gentleman.

The room was shabby but clean. On the table lay the remains of a cold meal that Lucas had had sent up from a delicatessen.

"Anything new, Inspector?"

"Anybody at home across the way?"

The room had been chosen for its strategic position; you could see straight into the two rooms of the Hôtel Beauséjour that the Poles occupied.

In this heat all the windows stood wide open, including the window of another room, which revealed a young girl asleep and scantily clad.

"Well, well, Lucas! Looks like you don't find your job too boring . . ."

A pair of field glasses on a chair gave evidence that Lucas attended to his work conscientiously and missed no detail, however slight.

"At the moment," said the sergeant, "there are two of them in the rooms, but there'll be only one in a minute. The man's getting dressed. He stayed in bed all morning, as usual."

"That's The Beard?"

"Yes. There were three of them for lunch: The Beard, the woman, and One-Eye. One-Eye left as soon as he'd eaten. Then The Beard got up and began to dress . . . Well! He's just put on a clean shirt. That doesn't happen very often."

Maigret came to the window to take his turn watching. The hairy giant was knotting his tie. The white shirt made an unexpected and therefore all the more dazzling splotch in the gray room.

You could see the man's lips move as he looked at himself in the mirror. Behind him the blond woman was cleaning up, gathering gray papers and rolling them into a ball, turning off the alcohol stove, dusting the frame of a bright-colored picture on the wall.

"If only we knew what they're saying!" Lucas sighed. "There are times when it drives me crazy. I watch them talking and talking and they never stop. They wave their arms around and I can't even guess what it's all about."

"The limitless resources of the police," said Maigret dryly, "do not include a lip reader who knows Polish."

"It gets on my nerves. I'm beginning to understand the torture it must be to be deaf. I'm beginning to see why people afflicted that way are generally so cranky."

"Don't talk so much! Do you think the woman will stay there?"

"This isn't the time she usually goes out. And if she meant to, she would have put on her gray suit."

Olga was wearing the same dark wool dress in which she had done her marketing that morning. While she cleaned up her bohemian establishment, she kept smoking a cigarette without ever taking it from her lips, in the fashion of the true smoker who needs tobacco from morning till night.

"She never talks," Maigret observed.

"This isn't the time she does that, either. It's in the evenings that she gets to talking, when they're all gathered around her. Or a few times when she's alone with the one I call Spinach—which doesn't happen very often. Either I'm badly mistaken or she has a weakness for Spinach. He's the best-looking of the lot."

It was a strange sensation to be in an unknown room like this, to look into the lives of people and come to know their smallest gestures.

"You're getting as snoopy as a concierge, Lucas."

"That's what I'm here for, isn't it? I can even tell you that the little girl over there—the one who's sleeping so soundly—was making love last night until three in the morning with a young man with an Ascot tie who left at dawn, undoubtedly so he could get into his family's house unnoticed—— Hold on! Now The Beard's leaving."

"Look at that, will you! He's practically elegant!"

"You might say so. But he looks more like a foreign wrestler than a man of the world."

"Well, let's say a wrestler who's doing good business," Maigret conceded.

No good-by kiss across the way. The man just went—that is, he disappeared from the part of the room visible from the police observatory.

A little later he emerged onto the sidewalk and set off toward Place de la Bastille.

"Derain will pick him up," Lucas announced, sitting there like a huge spider at the center of its web. "But he knows he's being followed. He won't do anything but walk around and maybe pick up a drink somewhere."

As for the woman, she had taken a road map out of a drawer and spread it on the table.

Ozep couldn't have taken a taxi, Maigret calculated; he must have come by subway, in which case he should arrive at any moment. "*If* he's coming . . ." he corrected himself.

And he did come. They saw him arrive, hesitate, wander up

and down the sidewalk, while the detective trailing him displayed great interest in a fish stall on Rue Saint Antoine.

Seen from above like this, the tiny Pole seemed even thinner, even more insignificant. Maigret experienced, for a moment, a pang of remorse. He could hear the poor devil's voice repeating a hundred times, in involved explanation, his famous "Monsieur Maigrette . . ."

He was hesitating; that was obvious. He seemed even to be afraid, to stare around him with a visible anguish.

"Do you know what he's looking for?" the inspector asked Lucas.

"The little pale fellow? No. Maybe some money to get into the hotel?"

"He's looking for me. He's saying to himself that I must be somewhere around and if by some miracle I've changed my mind . . ."

Too late to change now; Michael Ozep had plunged into the dark hallway of the hotel. They could follow him in their minds. He would be climbing the stairs, reaching the second floor. . . .

"He's still stalling," Maigret announced. The door should have opened before this. "He's on the landing. He's going to knock. He's knocked—look!"

The blond girl trembled, shoved the map, with an instinctive movement, back in the dresser, and went toward the door. For a moment they could see nothing. The two were in the invisible part of the room. Then suddenly the woman appeared. Something about her had changed. Her steps were fast, decisive. She went straight to the window, closed it, then drew the dark curtains.

Lucas turned to the inspector with a quizzical smile. "Think of that!" he laughed. But his smile faded as he noticed that Maigret was far more concerned than he had expected.

"What time is it, Lucas?"

"Three-ten."

"In your opinion, what are the chances that one of the gang will come back to the hotel in the next hour?"

"I doubt it. Unless, as I was telling you, Spinach, if he knows The Beard is out of the way. You don't look very happy about things."

"I don't like the way she closed that window."

"Are you afraid for your little Pole?"

Maigret made no answer.

"Have you thought," Lucas went on, "that we haven't any real proof that he is in that room? It's true we saw him go into the hotel. But he might perfectly well have gone to some other room, while somebody else came——"

Maigret shrugged his shoulders and sighed.

"WHAT TIME IS IT, LUCAS?"

"Three-twenty."

"Do you know what's going to happen?"

"Do you want to go over and see what's happening across the way?"

"Not yet. But I'm probably going to make a fool of myself . . . Where can you telephone?"

"In the next room. He's a tailor who does piecework for one of the big houses, so he has to have a phone."

"Go to your tailor, then. Try not to let him listen in. Telephone the chief, and tell him I want him to send me twenty armed men at once. They're to spread a cordon around the Hôtel Beauséjour and wait for my signal."

Lucas's expression indicated the seriousness of this order, so out of character for Maigret, who usually laughed at police mobilization. "You think there'll be dirty work going on?"

"If it hasn't already gone on . . ."

His eyes remained fixed on the window, on the filthy glass panes, on the crimson velvet curtains of the time of Louis Philippe.

When Lucas came back from the telephone, he found the inspector still in the same place, still frowning thoughtfully.

"The boss says please be careful. There was a detective killed only last week, and now if there should be another accident——"

"Shut up, will you?"

"Do you think that Stan the Killer——"

"I don't think anything! I've thought so much about this case since this morning that I've got a headache. Now I'm satisfied just to have impressions; and if you want to know, I have the impression that some disagreeable things are happening or are about to happen. What time is it?"

"Twenty-three after."

In the neighboring room the young girl was still asleep, her mouth open, her legs bent back. Higher up, on the fifth or sixth floor, somebody was trying to play an accordion, incessantly repeating, with the same false notes, the same fox-trot refrain.

"Do you want me to go over?" Lucas suggested.

Maigret gave him a harsh look, as if his subordinate had reproached him for lack of courage. "Just what do you mean by that?"

"Nothing. I can't help seeing you're worried about what may be going on over there, and I thought I could go and check——"

"And you think I'd hesitate to go myself? You're forgetting one thing: Once we're over there, it's too late. If we go and find nothing, we'll never pin anything on that gang. That's why I'm hesitating . . . If only that wench hadn't closed the window!" He suddenly lifted his eyebrows. "Tell me: The other times, when she's been alone with a man, she's never closed the window, has she?"

"Never."

"Then she hadn't any suspicion of your presence here."

"She probably took me for just another foolish old man."

"So it isn't the girl who had the idea of closing the window, but the character who came in."

"Ozep?"

"Ozep or somebody else. It's the one who came in who told the girl to close the window before he showed himself."

He took his hat from the chair, emptied his pipe, scraped the bowl with his index finger.

"Where are you going, Chief?"

"I'm waiting for our men to get here . . . Look! There are two of them by the bus stop. And I recognize some others in that parked taxi . . . If I stay inside five minutes without opening that window, you'll come in with our men."

"You have your gun?"

A few moments later Lucas could see Maigret crossing the street, could see Detective Janvier notice him and break off his task of wiping the tables on the terrace.

After what seemed a miraculously short interval, the window across the way opened. Maigret signaled to his sergeant to join him.

From across the street Lucas had gathered that the room was empty save for the inspector. He stumbled up a dark staircase through the stench of bad cooking and worse plumbing and entered the room, only to start back as he found the body of a woman stretched out at his feet.

"Dead, of course," Maigret grunted.

It was as if the murderer had wished to leave his signature on his crime. The woman's throat had been cut, as with all the other victims of Stan. There was blood everywhere.

The bright picture on the wall turned out, on closer inspection, to be a portrait of Olga—even blonder, even more fresh-skinned than she had been in life. Lucas looked from the lushly alluring portrait to the unappetizing sight on the floor. He felt oddly like a drinking man who sees a bottle of fine brandy smashed.

"It was your Pole?"

Maigret shrugged his shoulders, still standing rooted in the middle of the room.

"Shall I give his description to our men so they can see that he doesn't leave the hotel?"

"If you wish."

"I'd like to put a man on the roof, just in case——"

"Go ahead."

"Shall I call the chief?"

"In a minute."

It was no easy job to talk with Maigret when he was like this. Lucas tried to put himself in his shoes. Maigret himself had said that he'd make a fool of himself. But this was worse than looking foolish. He had mobilized a large body of police when it was too late, when the crime had already been committed under Maigret's very eyes—almost with his consent, since he'd been the one who had sent Ozep into the Hôtel Beauséjour.

"And if any of the gang come back, shall I arrest them?"

An affirmative nod. Or rather a gesture of indifference. And at last Lucas went out.

"WHERE'S MAIGRET?" the chief demanded of Lucas before he was halfway out of his car.

"In the room. Number Nineteen on the second floor. The people in the hotel don't know about it yet."

A few minutes later the director of the Police Judiciaire found Maigret sitting in a chair in the middle of the room, two steps from the body.

"Well, my friend! It looks to me as though we were in a pretty fix!"

For answer he received a grunt.

"So the notorious killer was none other than the little man who offered you his services! You must admit, Maigret, you might have been somewhat less trustful; Ozep's attitude was, to say the least, suspicious . . ."

A heavy vertical furrow seamed Maigret's brow and his jaws jutted out, giving his whole face a striking quality of power.

"You think he hasn't managed to slip out of the hotel yet?"

"I'm sure of it," the inspector replied, as if he attached not the least importance to the matter.

"You haven't searched the hotel?"

"Not yet."

"You think he'll let himself be captured easily?"

Then Maigret's gaze detached himself slowly from the window, shifted toward the director.

"If I'm wrong, the man will try to kill as many people as he can before he's arrested. If I'm not wrong, things will take care of themselves."

"I don't understand, Maigret."

"I tell you again, Chief: I can be wrong. Anybody can be wrong. In that case, I beg your pardon, because there's going to be trouble. The way this case seems to have solved itself doesn't satisfy me. There's something that doesn't fit, I can feel it. If Ozep was Stan, there was no reason why . . ." His voice trailed off.

"You're staying here, Maigret?"

"Pending further instructions, yes."

"Meanwhile, I'll go see what our men are doing outside."

They had arrested Spinach when, as Lucas had foreseen, he had come to pay his call on the young woman. When they told him that Olga had been killed, he turned pale, but he showed no reaction when they spoke of Ozep.

When this arrest was announced to Maigret, he merely mumbled, "What's it to me?" and resumed his strange tête-à-tête with the dead woman.

A half hour later it was One-Eye's turn to come home and be arrested on the threshold. He submitted impassively, but when they told him of the woman's death, he tried to break free from his handcuffs and leap upstairs.

"Who did it?" he shouted. "Who killed her? One of you, wasn't it?"

"It was Ozep, alias Stan the Killer."

The man quieted down as if by magic. He frowned as he repeated, "Ozep?"

"You aren't going to tell us you didn't know your boss's real name?"

It was the chief in person who conducted this hasty questioning in a corridor, and he had the impression that a faint smile crossed the prisoner's lips.

Then came another of the gang, the one they called The Chemist. He simply answered all questions with an air of absolute confusion, as if he had never heard of the woman or of Ozep or of Stan.

Maigret was still upstairs, mulling over the same problem, hunting for the key that would at last enable him to understand what had happened.

"All right . . ." he murmured when Lucas told him of the arrest of The Beard, who had begun by raging like a fiend and ended by bawling like a calf.

Suddenly he raised his head. "Do you notice something, Lucas? That's four that they've arrested, and not one of them's put up any real resistance. Whereas a man like Stan——"

"But since Stan is Ozep——"

"Have you found him?"

"Not yet. We had to let all the accomplices come home before we turned the hotel upside down. If they got a whiff of anything wrong, they'd never come into the mousetrap. Now that we have almost all of them, the big boss is laying siege to the establishment. Our men are downstairs and they're going to go through everything."

"Listen, Lucas . . ."

The sergeant had been about to leave. He paused, feeling for Maigret something akin to pity.

"One-Eye is not Stan. Spinach is not Stan. The Beard is not Stan. But I'm convinced that Stan lived in this hotel and was the focus around which the others gathered."

Lucas thought it better to say nothing. Let the inspector have his monomania.

"If Ozep was Stan, he had no reason to come here to kill an accomplice. If he was not Stan . . ."

Suddenly Maigret rose, crossed to the wall and pulled down

the brightly colored picture of Olga. He tore away the tape that framed it, revealing lines of lettering above and below the face. He handed it to Lucas.

The sergeant knew enough English to make out both the line above:

REAL LIFE DETECTIVE CASES

and the lines below:

THE PRETTY POLE AND THE
TERROR OF TERRE HAUTE

Maigret was smiling now. "Vanity," he said. "They can't ever resist it. They had to buy the magazine when they saw it on the stands, and she had to frame the picture.

"I knew I'd seen her face before. I do remember the case roughly. I kept some clippings on it. Very similar to ours. In the Middle West of America, four or five years ago. A gang attacking lonely farms, cutting throats . . . just like ours . . . and they had a woman leader. The American press took great pleasure in describing her atrocities."

"Then Stan . . . ?"

". . . was Olga. Almost certainly. I'll be positive in an hour, now that I know what to look for in the office. Are you coming with me, Lucas?"

"But Ozep?" Lucas asked as they settled back in the cab.

"It's Ozep I especially want to look up. That is, I'm hoping I'll find something about him. If he killed this woman, he must have had a motive . . . Listen, Lucas: When I wanted to send him to the others, he agreed at once. But when I gave him an errand to the woman, he refused, and I was forced to use pressure, even to threaten him. In other words, the rest of the gang did not know him—*but the woman did.*"

It took a good half hour to find the clippings in question. Order was not Maigret's dominant attribute.

"Read this! Always allowing for the exaggeration of the American press—they like to give the readers their money's worth. 'The Female Fiend . . .' 'The Deadly Pole . . .' 'Girl, 23, Heads Murder Gang . . .'"

The press reveled in the exploits of the Polish girl and furnished many proofs of her photogenic qualities.

At eighteen Stephanie Polintskaja was already known to the Warsaw police. Around this time she met a man who married her and strove to curb her evil instincts. She had a child by him. One day the man came home from work to find that his wife had vanished with all the money and jewelry. The child's throat had been cut.

"You know who that man was?" Maigret asked.

"Ozep?"

"Here's his picture, and a good likeness. You understand now? Stephanie, nicknamed Stan, ran wild in America. How she escaped the American prisons I do not know. In any case she took refuge in France, surrounded herself with a fresh lot of brutes, and took up her old career.

"Her husband learns from the papers that she is in Paris, that the police are on her trail. Does he want to rescue her once more? I doubt it. I'm rather inclined to think that he wants to make sure that the detestable murderess of his child shall not escape punishment. That's why he offers me his services. He hasn't the guts to work alone. He's too much of a weakling. He needs the police to help him. And then, this afternoon, I force his hand . . .

"Face to face with his former wife, what can he do? Kill or be killed! She certainly would not hesitate to destroy the only man outside the gang who could testify against her.

"So he killed . . . And do you want to know what I think? I'm betting that they'll find him somewhere in the hotel, more or less seriously wounded. After muffing two attempts at suicide,

it would amaze me if he muffed the third. Now you can go back
to the hotel and——"

"No use!" It was the chief's voice. "Stan the Killer hanged
himself in a vacant room on the sixth floor. Good riddance!"

"He made it," Maigret sighed. "Poor devil!"

"You're sorry for him?"

"Indeed I am. Especially since I'm somewhat responsible for
his death . . . I don't know if it means I'm getting old, but I
certainly took long enough to find the solution——"

"What solution?" the director asked suspiciously.

"The solution to the whole problem!" Lucas intervened happily.
"The inspector has reconstructed the case in all its details."

"That so, Maigret?"

"It is . . . You know, if you keep mulling over the same question . . . I don't think I've ever been so mad at myself in my life.
I felt that the solution was there, within reach, that just one little
touch . . . And you all kept buzzing around me like horseflies,
telling me about arrests that didn't mean a thing . . . And then
I remembered the American detective magazine and the woman's
face on the cover . . ."

Maigret took a deep breath, loaded his pipe, and asked Lucas
for matches. The afternoon vigil had used up all his own.

"What do you say, Chief? It's seven o'clock. Suppose we three
settle down to a nice glass of beer? Provided that Lucas gets rid
of his wig and makes himself respectable again."

The Old Lady of Bayeux

"SIT DOWN, MADEMOISELLE." Maigret sighed as he regretfully set aside his pipe.

And he again looked at the prosecutor's note and read: "A family matter. Please hear what Cécile Ledru has to say; but observe the utmost discretion in acting on it."

This was at Caen, in the period when Maigret had been sent down there to reorganize the district constabulary. He could not get used to this grasping, secretive Norman province; he felt hampered, confined, and missed the freedom of action he had enjoyed in Paris.

This note, for instance: "A family matter . . . the utmost discretion . . ." Did this mean that he was once more going to run up against the family of some high official or important personage of the district? It was incredible how many provincial big guns had cousins and brothers-in-law and sisters-in-law who had to be handled gently by the police!

"I'm listening, Mademoiselle Ledru."

She was something to look at, this Mademoiselle Cécile, almost too good-looking—an effect heightened by the mourning that poetically emphasized her naturally pale complexion.

"Your age?"

"Twenty-eight."

"Profession?"

"I suppose it would be best to explain everything to you, so that you can understand my position. I was an orphan, and I started out in life, at the age of fifteen, as a maid of all work. I was still wearing pigtails, and I didn't know how to read or write."

Maigret suppressed his astonishment. This was an amazing beginning for one who now possessed so marked an air of distinction.

"Please go on."

"I happened to secure employment with Madame Croizier, at Bayeux. You've heard of her?"

"I confess I haven't." These provincials! Always assuming that the whole world knows their local characters!

"I'll tell you more about her later. She became very fond of me. She induced me to study and make something of myself. Then she kept me with her, no longer as a servant, but as a companion. She asked me to call her Aunt Joséphine."

"So you live in Bayeux with Madame Joséphine Croizier?"

The girl's eyes clouded over with tears. "That's all over now," she said, drying her eyes with a handkerchief. "Aunt Joséphine died yesterday, here in Caen. That's why I came to see you. To tell you about the murder and——"

"Just a moment! You're sure that Madame Croizier was murdered?"

"I swear it."

"You were there?"

"No."

"Someone told you?"

"My aunt herself!"

"I beg your pardon? Your aunt *told* you that she had been murdered?"

"Please, Inspector! I am not suffering from delusions; I know very well what I'm saying. My aunt has told me time and again that if anything should happen to her in the house on Rue des Récollets, my first duty should be to demand an investigation into——"

"Just a moment. What is this 'house on Rue des Récollets'?"

"The home of her nephew, Philippe Deligeard. Aunt Joséphine had come to Caen for several weeks to have her teeth attended to. At sixty-eight, she was having trouble with them for the first time. She was staying with her nephew, and I had remained at Bayeux because Philippe doesn't care for me at all."

On a scrap of paper Maigret jotted down "Philippe Deligeard." "How old is this nephew?"

"Forty-four or five."

"Profession?"

"He has none. He had a fortune—his wife's—but I believe that for several years that fortune has been only a memory. Nevertheless, he still keeps up a large house on Rue des Récollets, with cook, butler, and chauffeur. Philippe often came to Bayeux to beg his aunt to lend him money."

"And did she?"

"Never! She used to tell her nephew he had only to be patient and wait for her death."

As the young woman talked on, Maigret mentally arranged one of his habitual résumés:

First of all, there lived in Bayeux, in one of those quiet streets near the cathedral where the sound of a footstep makes the curtains tremble in every window, a Madame Joséphine Croizier, widow of Justin Croizier.

Now the story of her fortune was at once macabre and droll. Croizier, a mere law clerk when he married, was a monomaniac on the subject of insurance. His hobby was to spend his time signing policies with every possible company, to the scornful amusement of all concerned.

For the first and last time in his life he took the boat to Southampton. It was a rough crossing. A lurch of the ship hurled him against a bulkhead and cracked his skull open; his widow, shortly thereafter, was astonished to receive a million francs from divers insurance companies.

From that time on Joséphine Croizier's only amusements, in her gloomy house in Bayeux, were to look after this constantly growing fortune and to spend whole afternoons chatting with her protégée, Cécile Ledru. She succeeded so well in the first of these occupations that she was rumored to be worth four or five million francs.

Her sister's son, Philippe Deligeard, had started off elegantly by marrying the daughter of a rich dealer in horses. He had furnished a magnificent mansion, renowned as one of the show places of Caen. But his investments had proved as unfortunate as his aunt's had been lucky; and it was rumored that he had been living for three or four years on credit, borrowing money at high interest against his future inheritance from his aunt.

"In short, Mademoiselle Cécile, the only serious basis for your accusation is that Philippe needed money badly, and his aunt's death provides him with it?"

"I already told you that Madame Croizier herself always said that if she should die on Rue des Récollets——"

"Pardon me, but you must know how much the fears of old ladies are worth as evidence. Now, about the actual facts of the case?"

"My aunt died yesterday, around five in the afternoon. They're trying to claim that she had a heart attack!"

"Did she have heart trouble?"

"Nothing to die of."

"Were you in Bayeux at this time?"

It seemed to Maigret, though it might have been a misleading impression, that the young lady showed a certain hesitation in answering.

"No . . . I was here in Caen."

"I thought that you had not accompanied Joséphine Croizier on this trip?"

"That's right. But by bus it's only a half hour from Bayeux to Caen. I came in to do a little shopping."

"And you didn't try to see your aunt, as you call her?"

"I stopped by the house on Rue des Récollets."

"At what time?"

"Around four. They told me that Madame Croizier had gone out."

"Who told you that?"

"The butler."

"After asking his employers?"

"No. On his own."

"Then we must believe either that it was true, or that he'd been given his instructions beforehand."

"That's what I thought."

"Then where did you go?"

"Downtown. I had a lot of little things to do. Then I went back to Bayeux, and this morning, when I read the Caen paper, I learned of my aunt's death."

"Curious . . ."

"I beg your pardon?"

"I say it's curious. At four in the afternoon, when you call at Rue des Récollets, you're told that your aunt is out. You go back to Bayeux, and the next morning you learn in the paper that your aunt died only a few minutes, an hour at most, after your visit. Is it correct that you've requested a police investigation, Mademoiselle Cécile?"

"Yes, Inspector. I haven't any fortune, but I'd gladly give the little I have to discover the truth and punish the guilty."

"Just a moment. Speaking of the state of your finances, may I ask if you stand to inherit from Joséphine Croizier?"

"I'm certain that I won't. I myself drew up her will, and I positively refused to accept anything whatsoever. Otherwise no one would have believed how truly disinterested my affection has been, during the years I have devoted to my benefactress."

She was almost too good to be true. Seek as he would, Maigret could not find the chink in her armor. "So you're left without a penny?"

"I didn't say that, Inspector. I received a salary as Madame Croizier's companion. Since I had no expenses, I was able to put away a nice little nest egg that will see me through for a while—though I'm willing to spend every sou of it to avenge my aunt."

"May I ask one more question? Philippe is the heir, isn't he? Now supposing it's proved he killed his aunt—then he won't be allowed to inherit. What will become of the millions?"

"They will go to institutions for the protection of young girls."

"Madame Croizier was interested in that sort of charity?"

"She felt a pity for young girls who live alone; she knew the dangers that surround them. . . ."

"She was very strait-laced?"

Cécile hesitated a moment, thinking it over. "Very much so."

"A trifle fanatical on the subject?"

"Almost . . ."

"Thank you, mademoiselle."

"You are going to make an investigation, aren't you?"

"I'll check up on the situation, and if it seems necessary . . . By the way, where can I find you?"

"My aunt's body is lying in the house on Rue des Récollets. Until the funeral—that will be two days from now, here in Caen —I'll be there with her most of the time."

"In spite of Philippe?"

"We don't speak to each other, and I don't so much as set foot in the rest of the house. I pray and I cry a little. . . . At night, I'm staying at the Hôtel Saint Georges."

MAIGRET FINISHED HIS PIPE while his little eyes studied the enormous gray house, the carriage gate with its copper ring, the ornate entrance court with its bronze candelabras.

It was almost twenty-four hours since the girl's visit. It had taken Maigret that long to clear up enough of the details of his reorganization to allow him to take charge of the investigation in person; any other inspector in Caen, he feared, might take the prosecutor's request for discretion too seriously. And discretion and all, he felt in his bones that this was going to be his kind of case—even though he had a sinking feeling that it would be what he called a No-Pipe Case—an investigation conducted in scenes of such respectability that the inspector could not decently keep his hay burner in his mouth.

That was why he stole a few last puffs before going in, watching the people who came and went: ladies in black, gentlemen formally garbed—all of the *haute bourgeoisie* of Caen, in short, come to pay their respects.

"This'll be a cheerful party!" he sighed as he finally tapped his pipe against his heel. And he went in like the rest, passed by the silver tray full of visiting cards, reached the end of a blue and white tiled hall, and beheld, beyond a large door draped with black, the coffin—surrounded by flowers, by candles, by black silhouettes, standing and kneeling.

The odor of burning wax and chrysanthemums was in itself enough to establish the atmosphere. Then the whisperings, the handkerchiefs dabbing at the mourning nostrils, that great air of dignity that people assume only before justice and death. . . .

Cécile Ledru was there in a corner, kneeling on a *prie-dieu*, her face covered by a black veil transparent enough to reveal her composed features, and the movement of her lips as the beads of a jade rosary slipped through her fingers.

A man clad all in black, his eyes reddened, his features distorted, kept watching Maigret as though wondering what right he had there. The inspector went up to him. "Monsieur Philippe

Deligeard? I'm Inspector Maigret. If you could let me see you alone for a moment . . ."

Maigret had the impression that the man cast a nasty look at the girl before leaving the black-draped room. "Come with me, monsieur. My office is on the next floor."

A marble staircase with a beautiful iron railing. On the wall of the landing a genuine Aubusson tapestry. Then an enormous office, with Empire furnishings, with three windows that opened on a park larger than seemed possible here in the midst of the city.

"Please sit down. I imagine that girl is still continuing her machinations and that I owe the pleasure of this visit to her?"

"You refer to Mademoiselle Cécile Ledru?"

"I do indeed refer to that conspirator from belowstairs who contrived, for a brief space of time, to exert an undue and unfortunate influence upon my aunt. A cigar?"

"No, thank you. You say 'for a brief space of time.' Should I take it that this influence didn't last?"

Maigret had no need to study Philippe Deligeard closely. Elegantly dressed even in his mourning, he was the perfect type to be found in every provincial city: the rich bourgeois, keeping up an impressive establishment, insisting above all on decorum, on the precise cut of clothes, the telling details of speech and manner that distinguished him from the common run of mortals.

"You understand, Inspector, how extremely painful, not to say disagreeable, it is to me to receive, in such sorrowful moments, the visit of a policeman. Nevertheless, I shall answer your questions. I want this affair to be cleared up, and I want to see Cécile receive the punishment she so well deserves."

"Which is . . . ?"

"As your previous question proves, you understand that my aunt was not ultimately deceived by the hypocritical manners of that girl or by her supposedly disinterested devotion. As evidence I may adduce the fact that when my aunt came to spend a month with us here, we suggested that she might bring her companion with her; the house is large enough. And she flatly refused, telling us in confidence that she had had enough of the girl and was looking for a way to get rid of her. All that she feared was that, if she broke off the relationship too brutally, Cécile might try to seek some revenge."

Maigret could not help it. It was the general atmosphere that forced him to murmur, with an irony his host overlooked, "How wicked and deceitful people are!"

"Sooner or later, therefore, my aunt would have made a clean break with this creature, who had even tried to cause trouble between my aunt and me."

"She did?"

"Claiming, among other things, that I had mistresses. Now as man to man, Inspector, you'll admit that at my age and in my situation it's natural to . . . oh, discreetly, of course, like any man of the world. . . . But of course my poor aunt, with her fixation on purity, couldn't understand that. You can't talk with old people about this sort of thing."

"Cécile told her?"

"How else could my aunt have learned it? But it was an unwise move; that treacherous girl saw her own maneuver rebound against her. When my aunt learned that her chaste companion was receiving, under her very roof, secret visits from a young man of whom the least that can be said is that his family is not of the best . . ."

"Cécile had a lover?" If Maigret's indignation was not actual, it was admirably played. And he took advantage of it to slip his pipe from his pocket with the most innocent air, as though he had completely forgotten the sumptuous décor that surrounded him and the Havana cigars awaiting him on the desk.

"For the last two years! It's two years now that they've been meeting almost every night. His name is Jacques Mercier. He and a friend have some sort of transportation business. And it's worth observing that his parents went through bankruptcy several years ago."

"Would you believe it! And you told this to your aunt?"

"Of course. Why shouldn't I? Wasn't it my duty?"

"Naturally."

"That was when my aunt finally made up her mind to get rid of Cécile. But the fear of some attempt at revenge still made her hesitate. That's why I suggested to my aunt that she should henceforth stay with us. I would have placed the entire second floor of our home at her disposal."

"And when were these questions discussed?"

"Why . . . the day before yesterday. . . ."

"And a decision was reached?"

"Not formally. But the principle was established."

"Nevertheless, I don't imagine that you'd accuse Cécile of having murdered your aunt?"

Philippe lifted his head abruptly and looked at Maigret with utter astonishment. "But there's no question of murder! That girl must be as insane as she is vicious if she's been telling you such absurd fantasies. My aunt died of a heart attack. The medical examiner expressly stated as much in his certificate."

"In short, you do not accuse Cécile of the murder of your aunt?"

"I certainly would if I were not sure that my aunt had died a natural death. As it is, however, if this girl continues to spread such stories about us, I shall be forced to bring suit against her for slander."

"One question, Monsieur Deligeard: Your aunt died around five o'clock, didn't she?"

"A few minutes after five, yes. Or so my wife tells me; I was not here myself."

"All right. Now, around four o'clock, Joséphine Croizier was not in this house?"

"Every day at four she had an appointment with her dentist. She was having several bridges fitted—a long and difficult job."

"Do you know what time your aunt came back to the house?"

"Around five, they tell me. It was almost immediately after her return that she had the attack; she died before anyone could do anything for her."

"The attack happened in her bedroom?"

"Yes. The Louis XIV room on the second floor."

"Your wife was up there with her?"

"She went up as soon as my aunt opened her door and called for help."

"May I ask where you were?"

"I imagine, Inspector, that these questions are not part of a formal investigation? That, I warn you, I will not tolerate."

"Of course not. This is just so we can prove to that nuisance of a girl that there's nothing to investigate."

"Ah . . . certainly. . . . I must have been at my club. I generally leave here around four-thirty or quarter of five, and walk through the city to get a little exercise. Around five I settle down to bridge, and at seven-thirty the car comes to bring me home for dinner."

"You received the news by telephone at your club?"

"Exactly."

"And when you got home . . . ?"

"My aunt was dead and the doctor was already here."

"Your family doctor?"

"No; he lives too far away. My wife called a doctor in the neighborhood, but it was too late for him to do anything."

"The servants?"

"Arsène, the chauffeur, had the day off. The butler is on duty on the main floor all afternoon. The cook must, I imagine, have been in the kitchen. Now is there anything more that you would like to know, Inspector? I owe a duty to those who have come to offer me their condolences, and I am expecting at any moment the presiding judge, who is also president of my club. I think the best thing that you can do is to give that girl a good warning. If she continues to spread these vile stories, I'll have a warrant out against her."

Philippe Deligeard must have wondered what could have

caused, in so solemn a moment, the odd smile on Maigret's lips. The inspector had, for some moments, been staring at the mirror over the fireplace, which reflected a curtained doorway. The curtain had moved several times, and once the inspector had glimpsed a pale face that could belong only to Madame Deligeard. He could not help speculating whether she had overheard her husband's man-to-man exposition of the life of a man of the world.

"Good day, Inspector. I dare hope that after these explanations I have taken the trouble to make, my mourning will no longer be disturbed by this stupid and indecent fiction. The butler will show you out."

Philippe rang, nodded curtly to the policeman, and moved off with dignified strides toward the curtained doorway.

A quarter of an hour later Maigret sat in the office of the Prosecutor for the Republic—a placid and ironic Maigret, regretfully fingering his pipe in his pocket; for the Caen prosecutor was not a man to allow smoking in his office.

"Well, Inspector? You heard the girl's story?"

"I also visited the scene of the death."

"What's your opinion? A lot of nonsense, isn't it?"

"On the contrary, I have the feeling that this poor old lady Joséphine Croizier was assisted on her way out of this world. But by whom? That's the question. . . . And there's one other question: Do you really want to find out?"

THE HÔTEL SAINT GEORGES was one of those little residential hotels that exist in every city—the hotels you never hear of unless someone sends you there, the hotels whose tenants are old people, priests, fanatically devout girls, in short everyone remotely connected with pious devotion, from beadles to candle manufacturers.

The lobby was furnished with rattan chairs. Maigret had been waiting there a good half hour. An old lady looked up from her embroidery from time to time to cast a glance of suspicious severity at the inspector, as the smoke of his pipe drifted up to form a bluish halo around the chandelier.

"You, my fine fellow, are waiting for the same person as I am," Maigret had wagered as soon as he saw a young man pacing up and down the lobby and consulting his watch at one-minute intervals.

Now, after a half-hour wait, the two men had come to know each other without exchanging a word. As the young man surveyed Maigret from head to foot, his thoughts were self-evident: "So this is the famous inspector Cécile was talking about! He looks harmless enough . . . plump, good-natured. . . . But there must be some news, since he's looked up Cécile at the hotel."

And for his part Maigret was thinking, "Not bad, this young Jacques Mercier! Quite a boy, in fact—maybe a little too much so. Not at all the proper young provincial. Looks as if he might have ideas of his own. Good features, wavy hair, bright eyes, fire in his veins. . . . Aha! Mademoiselle Cécile! It looks to me as if you liked contrasts, and as if your prudence might be a bit less pronounced at night."

When she came in, she first saw Jacques Mercier, and a smile lit up her face. But the young man pointed to the inspector, and she came up to him, frowning.

"You want to talk to me?" she asked. She did not seem pleased to meet Maigret in her lover's presence.

"I'd like to straighten out a few small matters. But this doesn't seem to me to be quite the right place. This hotel's so quiet you can hear the moths buzzing. Wouldn't you like to go out to a café for a moment?"

Cécile looked at Mercier. He nodded, and a little later the three of them were sitting in a bar, with a billiard game going on next to them.

"First of all, let me point out, Mademoiselle Cécile, that it wasn't very nice of you not to mention Monsieur Mercier to me."

"I felt he had nothing to do with the case, but I should have known Philippe would tell you all about him. What else did he say about me?"

"Very nasty things, as you might guess. I believe he's what they call a perfect man of the world, but he has a very sharp tongue. One beer, waiter! What are you drinking, Mademoiselle? Port? You too? Two ports."

Maigret relaxed on the moleskin banquette, his eyes mechanically following the billiard balls. As he smoked in little voluptuous puffs, he seemed to be savoring the gray, pervasive peace of provincial life.

"So this has been going on for two years?"

"It's two years since we met, if that's what you mean."

"And how long has it been since Monsieur Mercier fell into the habit of spending his nights in the old lady's house?"

"Over a year. . . ."

"It never occurred to you to get married?"

"The old lady, as you call her, would never have allowed it. Or rather, she would have regarded it as an act of treason against her. She was jealous of my affection. There was nobody else in her life but nephews whom she loathed; so she looked on me as the one thing belonging to her. It was for her sake that I concealed my relationship with Jacques, so as not to hurt her feelings."

She answered Maigret's questions docilely enough, while her companion occasionally raised his eyebrows, as though to suggest a trifle more discretion.

"Your turn, Monsieur Mercier."

"I don't see how I'm involved in——"

"Nobody's trying to involve you. Mademoiselle Cécile has asked the police to do a job, and you can help by answering questions. Philippe Deligeard asserts that your business isn't doing well. Is that true?"

"Well . . ."

"Is it true?"

"Answer him, Jacques!"

"It's true enough. I went into business with a friend, and we bought three used trucks to transport fish from the little ports on the Channel. Unfortunately, the trucks turned out to be in pretty bad shape, and what with all the repairs and——"

"When's it due?"

"When's what due?"

"Your going out of business?"

"The trucks haven't run for three days now, because the garage rent isn't paid."

"Thank you. Now Mademoiselle, would you tell me again what time you reached Rue des Récollets?"

"Day before yesterday? Around four . . . wasn't it, Jacques?"

"I beg your pardon; you were with her?"

"I brought her in my car and waited at the corner. It must have been five after four."

"You drove her from Bayeux?" Maigret looked severely at Cécile, who had told him that she came by bus. "All right. Now tell me, mademoiselle: when you learned of Joséphine Croizier's death from the paper, I imagine you asked Mercier to drive you back to Caen. What time did you reach Rue des Récollets?"

"Around nine-thirty in the morning."

"Then the old lady had been dead for a whole night. Will you tell me precisely what you saw?"

"What do you mean? First I saw the butler, then some men in the great hall, then Philippe Deligeard, who came up to me and sneered, 'I thought you'd come running!' Then I saw my aunt——"

"One moment. This is the part that interests me. You saw your aunt's body. Where?"

"In the coffin."

"So it was already in the coffin, but the lid hadn't been closed yet?"

"They closed it a little later. I saw them. The men I'd met in the hall were from the funeral parlor."

"So you recognized your aunt's face? You're certain of that?"

"Absolutely! What on earth are you thinking of?"

"You didn't notice anything abnormal?"

"Of course not. I was crying . . . I was very upset . . . I should have liked to be alone with her a little, but that wasn't possible. . . ."

"One last question: I know the main entrance to the house on Rue des Récollets. But I imagine there must be another?"

"There's a little door in the rear, on Rue de l'Echaudé. That's more of an alley than a street; there aren't any houses facing on it, just garden walls."

"If you go in by this door, can you get into the upper part of the house without going near the butler or the cook?"

"Yes. You take what they call the staircase; it leads to the second floor."

"How much do I owe you, waiter? Thank you, mademoiselle. And you too, Monsieur Mercier."

Maigret paid the bill and rose, more cheerful than the circumstances seemed to indicate.

A few minutes later, his pipe still in his mouth, he had entered Deligeard's club and made his way into the secretary's office. There he asked a number of questions and jotted down the answers detailedly in his notebook, with an ever-growing air of satisfaction.

"Now let me read this summary back to you. You say that you're certain you saw Philippe Deligeard arrive day before yesterday at five-fifteen . . . that's right? His three usual partners were waiting for him to round out the bridge game that regularly started at five. He took his place at the table. As soon as the cards were dealt he was called to the telephone. When he left the booth, he'd turned very pale, and announced that his aunt had just died at his home. . . . That's all; you can't think of anything more to add? Thank you. Good day, monsieur."

And Maigret shrugged his shoulders as he crossed through the solemn rooms where sad old men, sunk into the depths of their armchairs, dozed behind the screens of their newspapers.

DR. LIÉVIN, the neighborhood doctor who had been called in too late, was a very young man with bright red hair. He wore a white coat and was at the moment engaged in broiling a chop over the gas stove in his consulting room.

"Am I disturbing you, Doctor? You'll forgive me, but I need a few details concerning the death of Madame Croizier."

Liévin was a bare twenty-seven. He had just begun to practice in Caen; and, to judge from his office, he was not yet over-burdened with patients.

"I suppose, first of all, that you are the nearest doctor to the Deligeards' house?"

"Almost. I think I have a colleague on Rue des Minimes."

"Had you had any previous occasion to be called in by Monsieur Deligeard?"

"Never. As you realized when you came in, I've just begun my practice here and I don't have many patients. It was quite a surprise to me to be called in to one of the finest homes in the city."

"What time was it? Can you fix the time exactly?"

"With the most rigorous precision," Liévin smiled. "I have a little nurse who comes in every afternoon for my consultation hours; she leaves at five o'clock. She had just put on her hat and I was in the very act of kissing her when the phone rang."

"So it was five exactly. How long did it take you to reach Rue des Récollets?"

"Seven or eight minutes."

"The butler let you in and took you up to the second floor?"

"No, not exactly. The butler opened the door, but all at once a woman leaned over the staircase and called down, 'Come quickly, Doctor!' It was Madame Deligeard, and she herself showed me into the bedroom on the right——"

"Just a minute. The bedroom on the right . . . that would be a room with light blue hangings?"

"You're mistaken, Inspector. The room on the right is papered, not hung. Wall paper with yellow circles."

"Louis XIV furniture?"

"Pardon me. I know a little about periods, and I can state positively that the room on the right is Regency."

To the doctor's astonishment Maigret wrote all these apparently insignificant details down in his notebook. "All right. You're upstairs and it's about five-ten. Where's the body?"

"On the bed, of course."

"Undressed?"

"Naturally."

"I beg your pardon. This was at five-ten, and Joséphine Croizier was undressed. What was she wearing?"

"A nightgown and a robe."

"Outer clothing lying around?"

"I don't think so. . . . No; everything neat and in order."

"And no one there but Madame Deligeard?"

"Yes. She was extremely nervous. She described her aunt's attack; I realized that death must have been practically instantaneous. Nevertheless, I examined the dead woman and found that she had been in a greatly weakened condition; this must have been at least her tenth attack."

"Could you determine approximately the time of death?"

"That's automatic. . . . Within a minute or two, I'd place the death at four-fifteen."

The doctor recoiled in astonishment as Maigret leaped up and seized him by the shoulders. "What? Four-fifteen?"

"Why, yes. Madame Deligeard made no secret of the fact that she'd tried to get hold of two other doctors before falling back on me. That takes some time——"

"Four-fifteen!" Maigret repeated, rubbing his brow. "I don't want to offend you, Doctor, but . . . you're new at the game . . . Are you positive of what you're saying? Would you persist in this statement if a man's life were at stake?"

"I could only repeat——"

"All right. I believe you. But I ought to warn you that you'll almost certainly have to repeat this statement in court, and the lawyers'll do everything they can to break your testimony."

"They won't succeed."

"Have you anything else to tell me? What happened next?"

"Nothing. I signed the death certificate. Madame Deligeard insisted on paying me on the spot and gave me two hundred francs."

"Is that your usual fee?"

"Hardly. It was her idea; I didn't argue. She went with me halfway downstairs. The butler opened the door for me."

"And you didn't meet anyone else?"

"Not a soul."

THROUGH THE WINDOWS of the little house Maigret could see the family at dinner. "It can't be helped," he muttered, as he interrupted the domestic scene by pressing the doorbell.

The medical examiner was a little old man, half deaf, still holding his napkin in his hand. He led Maigret into an office reeking of cabbage soup and ringing with the clatter of knives and forks from the dining room.

"Did you know Monsieur and Madame Deligeard before you were called in to certify their aunt's death officially?"

"I've vaguely noticed Monsieur Deligeard around town. After all, he's a prominent man. But we didn't move in the same circles."

"When did you go to the house?"

"The city hall notified me around six-thirty. I reached Rue des Récollets before seven."

"You knew Madame Croizier?"

"No. The butler asked me to wait while he announced me to his master. Then Monsieur Deligeard took me up to the second floor and into a room done all in yellow——"

"You're sure it was a yellow room?"

"Absolutely. It struck me because my daughter wants a yellow room and my wife insists it isn't the right thing. I found that the old lady had died of a heart attack and I filled out the usual forms."

"She was undressed?"

"In her night clothes."

"No disorder in the room?"

"I didn't notice any."

"Did you meet anyone?"

"Not a soul. Why?"

"Finally, have you any idea of the time of death?"

"I wasn't paying much attention. . . . Between four and five, I'm sure."

"Thank you."

The smell of the soup had roused the inspector's appetite. He went to a restaurant noted for its Normandy sole and its tripe *à la mode de Caen*. Even the restaurant, like all the other scenes Maigret had visited that day, had something dusty and solemn about it—a sort of deliberate austerity.

Yet this was the sort of case that Maigret liked best: a dignified façade, venerable and decorous characters, every indication of virtue exaggerated to the point of boredom. And then it was up to Maigret to tear down that façade, to sniff around in the ruins and nose out at last the human beast, the most unforgivable of evils, the killer for profit.

He was taking it easy on this case. There was a certain malicious pleasure in proceeding slowly, in playing cat-and-mouse with the murderer. . . .

The prosecutor had repeated, "Do what you must, but be discreet! A slip could cost you dear . . . and me, too. Philippe Deligeard is a well-known man about town; he may have his debts, but he's received everywhere. And as for the girl—Cécile, as you call her—if you lay a hand on her, you'll have the press championing her as the victim of the capitalists. The watchword, Inspector, is discretion!"

And Maigret had murmured to himself disrespectfully, "All right, old lady! But nobody's going to get away with anything."

The tripe was tasty, and Maigret left the table in a state of bliss heightened by his inability to refuse the proprietor's calvados.

"Pretty soon I'll have it all straightened out," he promised himself. "And now, an interview with that butler. . . ."

The Deligeards' butler answered his ring and began to show him into the waiting room.

"No, my friend, it's you I want to talk to. You know who I am, don't you? What were you doing when I rang?"

"Coffee was being served in the kitchen."

"Then I'll have my coffee in there with you."

There was nothing for the butler to do in the face of this self-invitation but to lead Maigret to the kitchen and announce to the cook and the chauffeur, "The inspector would like a cup of coffee."

Arsène, the chauffeur, wore a very elegant gray uniform, now unbuttoned for kitchen informality. The cook was a very fat woman.

"Don't disturb yourselves on my account, friends. I could have called you down to headquarters, but it wasn't worth bothering you for such trifles. Don't button up, Arsène! Be comfortable. . . . By the way, how did you happen to have the day off the day before yesterday? Was it your regular day?"

"Not exactly. That morning the boss said out of a clear sky that I couldn't have my day off next week on account of a trip to the south, so I'd better take it then."

"Monsieur Philippe drove himself, then?"

"Yes. I didn't think he'd be needing the car, but I noticed he'd used it."

"How could you tell?"

"There were mud spots inside."

"It wasn't raining, so he must have gone to the country?"

"Well, around here, you see, the country starts right near the house. A few hundred yards and you're off the paved roads."

Maigret turned to the butler. "And where were you during the afternoon?"

"In the pantry, which is near the entrance hall. The day before yesterday I was polishing the silver."

"Can you tell me what time Madame Croizier went out?"

"A few minutes before four, the same as every day. Her appointment with the dentist was at four, and he's only a stone's throw away from here."

"She looked well?"

"She always did. She was a very well-preserved woman—very cheerful, not at all proud. She never went by without a word for us."

"Did she say anything in particular to you this time?"

"No. She just called out, 'See you later, Victor.' "

"She walked to the dentist's office?"

"Madame Croizier did not care for automobiles. Even when she went home to Bayeux, she always preferred to take the train."

"Could you tell me where the car was at that time?"

"No, monsieur."

"It wasn't in the garage?"

"No, monsieur. Monsieur and Madame went out in it immediately after lunch. They came back about an hour later, but they must have left the car outside. I should tell you it's never parked in this street—it's too narrow—but around the corner, where I can't see it when I open the door."

"So Monsieur and Madame, as you say, came back around three. One hour later, a little before four, Madame Joséphine Croizier went out. Then?"

"Mademoiselle Cécile called."

"At what time?"

"Four-ten. I told her that her aunt had left, and she went away."

"She didn't see anyone except you?"

"No one."

"And then?"

"Monsieur went out. It was four twenty-five. I noticed the time, because it was a little early for him."

"He wasn't carrying anything?"

"Not a thing."

"He was behaving normally?"

"I think so."

"Go on."

"I'd just begun on the knives. . . . Yes . . . that was all that happened then. And it was almost five when Madame Croizier came back."

"Still looking fine?"

"And in very good humor. She said to me as she went by that it's all wrong to talk about dentists as people who hurt you. . . ."

"She went up to her room?"

"Yes."

"Hers is the Louis XIV room?"

"Indeed it is."

"The yellow room, on the right?"

"Oh no! That's the Regency room. That's hardly ever used."

"What happened next?"

"I don't know. . . . Several minutes went by. Then Madame came down, all excited——"

"Just a moment. How many minutes went by?"

"About twenty. . . . At any rate, it was well after five when Madame asked me to call Monsieur at his club and tell him his aunt had had an attack."

"So you phoned him and told him?"

"Yes."

"That's all you said?"

"It's all I knew."

"Then you went upstairs?"

"No, none of us went upstairs. A young doctor came and Madame took him up. . . . It wasn't until seven that we were officially informed of Madame Croizier's death, and not till eight that we all saw her——"

"In the yellow room?"

"No! In the blue room."

A bell rang. Victor groaned, "It's Monsieur. He wants his tea."

And Maigret turned slowly toward the door.

WHEN HE WAS THROUGH at the house on Rue des Récollets,
Maigret found his way to the offices of Caen's leading daily newspaper, where he bought a copy of the previous day's paper.

Over a glass of beer in a sidewalk café he studied the paper
carefully, with particular attention to the obituary column, in
which Mademoiselle Cécile had learned the news of her aunt's
death.

Over a second beer he mediated. Suddenly he said aloud,
"Discretion!" Then he rose, paid his bill, flagged a taxi, and rode
to the outskirts of town, where the paved streets end.

"The prosecutor asks you to wait."

Maigret waited. The bench was hard and the hallway was dusty
in the Caen courthouse.

It was ten in the morning. A policeman had showed up early
at his *pension* (a poor substitute for Madame Maigret and the
apartment in Paris) with a terse summons from the prosecutor
requesting Maigret's presence at the office at ten sharp.

At ten minutes after ten he rose from his bench and approached
the attendant. "Is there someone in the prosecutor's office?"

"Yes. He's been in there since nine-thirty. It's Monsieur
Deligeard."

An odd smile drifted across Maigret's lips. Each time he passed
before a certain padded door, he heard a murmur of voices. And
each time the same smile crossed his lips again.

It was after ten-thirty when a bell summoned the attendant,
who returned to announce, "The prosecutor will see you now."

And Philippe Deligeard had not yet left. Maigret thrust his hot
pipe in his pocket and went in with a slow ponderousness that
was at least half assumed. It often struck Maigret's fancy,

especially when he was in a particularly good humor, to assume a deliberate air of stupidity—at which times he seemed clumsy, bumbling, and even fatter than usual.

"My respects to the prosecutor. A very good day to you, Monsieur Deligeard."

"Close the door, Inspector. You place me in an extremely delicate and disagreeable situation. What did I recommend to you yesterday?"

"Discretion, Monsieur Prosecutor."

"Did I not also tell you that I placed no reliance on the fables of that girl, that Cécile?"

"And you told me that Monsieur Deligeard was an important man in Caen and we had to be very careful how we handled things where he was involved." Maigret smiled blandly, looking out of the corner of his eye at Philippe.

In full mourning Monsieur Deligeard seemed even more solemn than the prosecutor. He affected an air of complete disinterest, not even turning toward the inspector.

The prosecutor glared ferociously at the inspector, as if he suspected the irony that lay behind this oafish affability. He seemed to have some trouble controlling his anger as he ordered, "Sit down! I detest people who pace about!"

"Gladly, Monsieur Prosecutor."

"Where were you at nine o'clock last night?"

"At nine? Let me think. . . . Why, I must have been at Monsieur Deligeard's."

"Without his knowledge! Behind his back! You were there under false pretenses; no search warrant had been issued to you!"

"I had a few questions to ask his servants."

"That is exactly why Monsieur Deligeard has come here to bring charges against you. Those charges, I am forced to admit, are completely justified. You have overstepped your rights. If you needed to question the servants, you should have notified their employer of the fact; that is elementary. You understand me?"

"Certainly, Monsieur Prosecutor." And Maigret maliciously

lowered his eyes like a petty civil servant caught in an error.

"That is not all! What follows is far more serious—so serious that I cannot yet foresee all the repercussions your actions will provoke in high places. After you had complaisantly listened to, solicited, and I may even say provoked malicious gossip from the servants, you left the house; but it was not long before you re-entered by another door. I suppose you do not deny this?"

Maigret sighed humbly.

"What key did you use to open the garden door? Was it perchance Cécile Ledru who lent it to you? I advise you to weigh carefully the consequences of your answer."

"I didn't have a key to the little door. I really wasn't even planning to go into the garden. I just wanted to know how they brought in the body. . . ."

"What's that?" Both the prosecutor and Philippe rose abruptly, one as pale as the other.

"I'll tell you all about that in a minute, if you want me to. But about the door: I saw that it had a childishly simple lock. Any honest pass key ought to be able to open it. I wanted to make sure, so I tried it. It was a dark night. The garden was deserted. I noticed that it wasn't far to the garage. Now, I didn't want to disturb Monsieur Deligeard for such a trifle, especially in his sorrow, so I just went over to look at the mud spots Arsène was talking about."

The prosecutor frowned. Philippe, his gloves in his hand, started to speak, but Maigret left him no opportunity.

"That's all. . . . I know I shouldn't have done it. I ask your pardon and I'll try to justify myself as best I can."

"You confess to a violation of the code! You, a police inspector——"

"I can't say how sorry I am, Monsieur Prosecutor. . . . If I hadn't been so careful not to disturb Monsieur Deligeard—I knew he'd just had his tea sent up—I might have asked him some questions——"

"That will do! I may add that I do not care for this tone of mockery you seem to feel you have the right to assume. I am forwarding today, to the Ministry of Police, Monsieur Deligeard's charges against you. I believe we may now, until further notice, consider this incident closed. I trust that I have given you every possible satisfaction."

"Thank you, my dear Prosecutor. This man's conduct has been an outrage. I assure you that it is only my regard for the reputation of the police that restrains me from taking even stronger measures."

The prosecutor received Monsieur Deligeard's hand with cordial warmth and hastened to show him to the door.

"Again, thank you. I'll be seeing you soon, I trust?"

"I'll be at the funeral tomorrow, Monsieur Deligeard, and I hope——"

Suddenly they heard Maigret's voice peacefully observing, "Monsieur Prosecutor for the Republic, I should like, if you'd allow, to ask this man one question. Just one."

The prosecutor frowned. Deligeard, already on the threshold, paused automatically, and Maigret murmured, "Could you tell me, monsieur, if you will go to Caroline's funeral?"

The prosecutor was astonished at the effect of these words. In one instant Philippe's face seemed to fall apart.

Still placid, too placid, Maigret closed the door.

"You can see that we aren't really through yet. I beg your pardon for detaining you, but I'm only afraid it won't be for long enough."

"Inspector——" the prosecutor began.

"Don't be afraid. This Caroline doesn't mean that I'm planning, as the papers say, to unveil the secrets of private life. She isn't a kept woman or a working girl seduced by Monsieur Deligeard. It's all perfectly respectable; she's his old nurse. . . ."

"I must ask you to explain . . ."

"As lucidly as I can without wasting your time and without showing you where it all happened. . . . I'll begin, if you wish, with The Mystery of the Yellow Room, which must surely bring back pleasant memories of your boyhood reading. And this yellow room was the basis of all my discoveries; or rather, it confirmed my suspicions and allowed me to proceed—— Stop looking at the door, Monsieur Deligeard! It's no use."

"I am waiting," the prosecutor sighed, playing with a letter opener.

"You must know that on the second floor of the house on Rue des Récollets, Madame Joséphine Croizier occupied the bedroom on the left, called the Louis XIV room, which had pale blue hangings. Now, at a few minutes to five, Joséphine Croizier entered the house in the best of health, exchanged a pleasantry or two with the butler, and went up to her room. Which is to say, the blue room.

"Now when Dr. Liévin answered the telephone summons at five-ten, he was shown into the bedroom on the right, the Regency room, which is furnished in a lovely yellow. And in this room the poor old lady lay, already undressed and in her night clothes, without even a trace of the disorder that follows a hasty undressing. What is your opinion?"

"Go on!" the lawyer said dryly.

"Nor was this the only mystery involved. Here's another: Young Dr. Liévin, who has only just come to the district and who treats poor people for a ten-franc consultation fee, is summoned to the elegant mansion of the Deligeards in preference to any other practitioner. He finds that the death took place at around four-fifteen. Who's lying? The doctor, or the butler who saw Madame Croizier come in a little before five? And if it's the butler, the dentist must be lying too; he states that at four-fifteen the old lady of Bayeux was in his office."

"I don't understand. . . ."

"Patience! I didn't understand it either, at first. Any more than I understood why Monsieur Deligeard, who left his house earlier than usual that day, did not reach his club until five-fifteen."

"Sometimes a man walks faster or slower. . . ." This defense came from the prosecutor; Deligeard, his face drained of color, sat motionless.

"Then answer this question, Monsieur Prosecutor. Monsieur Philippe had hardly reached the club when his butler phoned him that his aunt had had an attack. That was all the butler said, because it was as much as he knew. Then Monsieur Deligeard went back to the card room, shocked, and announced that his aunt had just died."

The prosecutor cast an unpleasant look at Philippe, who sat motionless.

"Now for the secondary questions: Why, on that particular day, had Monsieur Deligeard given his chauffeur the day off on the pretext of a coming trip? Coincidence? All right. Why does he take the car out at two in the afternoon, and then leave it outside? Where do he and his wife go between two and three?"

"To the bedside of a sick woman!" Philippe suddenly answered.

"To the bedside—exactly—of Caroline, of Caroline who lives on the outskirts of town, which accounts for the mud. And I can prove that that mud comes from in front of the lime kiln across from Caroline's house."

As if mechanically, Maigret had begun to load his pipe and pace up and down the office.

"We are confronted, my dear Prosecutor, with one of the basest, meanest crimes I have ever encountered—at the same time almost a perfect crime—a crime predicated on the assumption that there cannot possibly be more than a token investigation into a superficially plausible death of a leading citizen of a provincial town.

"Philippe Deligeard has never done a blessed thing in his life but marry a rich wife, live on a grand scale, and speculate with so little judgment that he lost her entire fortune. For three years he's been in desperate straits; and his only resource is his aunt, who refuses to help him.

"It's obvious. It's simple!"

"Monsieur Deligeard will not contradict me when I say that there were days, despite the grand life he led, when there wasn't a hundred francs of cash money in the house.

"You can't learn a profession or a trade at his age. You can't change your way of living overnight.

"The aunt is old. In spite of that disquieting girl Cécile Ledru, she won't disinherit her nephew—especially since my fine Cécile doesn't approve of it. But just to make sure, Philippe drops a hint to the old lady that the girl is somewhat less pure than the driven snow. . . .

"You're following me, Monsieur Prosecutor? You might say that the murder is already decided upon, out of sheer necessity: Joséphine Croizier has to die if the Deligeards are to go on living according to their tastes.

"On the other hand, if it's easy enough to push someone over the border line between life and death, it's a tough job to hide the cause of death from the doctors. Particularly in a case of inheritance, and above all in the provinces, poison is risky; it's the first thing the gossips will think of, and everybody knows that the Deligeards are penniless. Shooting's impossible . . . a knife leaves traces. . . .

"As I say, the murder is already decided upon. All that's lacking is opportunity—the opportunity to do away with the old lady with no risks.

"And then, all of a sudden, there's the opportunity.

"Philippe has an old nurse, Caroline, just about Madame Croizier's age, who lives alone in a house just outside of town and who has no relatives. She's had several heart attacks. Now the Deligeards get word that she's had another. They go to see her at two in the afternoon, and come back an hour later knowing that Caroline hasn't two hours to live.

"The arrangement of the house favors their plans, but still they're careful to overlook no detail.

"Madame Deligeard leaves at once by the back door, walks to

Caroline's—it isn't far—and holds her bedside vigil until the old nurse dies around four-fifteen.

"Philippe does not leave the house until his usual hour—a little earlier because of his impatience. He finds his car around the corner, drives to Caroline's, loads the body in the car, and brings his wife back with him.

"The two of them, still using the back door, bring the body into the house and set it up in the yellow room on the second floor.

"As far as the servants know, Madame Deligeard has not left the house; her husband is on his way to the club.

"They are in the house, waiting for the aunt to return. She must come soon. . . . She does, she enters her bedroom—the blue room—and is killed on the spot.

"All that is left is for Philippe to go to his club—by the back door, in his car—to create an alibi. He is to drive back in the car later, explaining his prompt return probably by saying that he took a taxi.

"The doctor is carefully chosen because he knows neither the house nor Joséphine Croizier. Madame shows him Caroline's body; he quite correctly diagnoses natural death and signs the certificate. The same business later with the medical examiner.

"Take the nurse's body back to her house late that night, and the job's done."

There was a silence. The prosecutor studied his letter opener as he asked, "What made you think of Caroline?"

"Logic! The two doctors could not possibly have examined the body of Joséphine Croizier. So I bought the next day's paper. I read the list of deaths. I was certain I'd find at least one old lady. I found her, I investigated, and when I learned her connection with the Deligeards, the case was as good as over. Her neighbors will testify to various comings and goings by car that day; they didn't think anything about it because they knew the old lady's former employers often came to see her. Possibly the one thing in his life that's to Philippe Deligeard's credit."

The silence was heavy. Then, with a sudden rap of the letter opener, the prosecutor asked hesitantly, "Do you confess, Philippe Deligeard?"

"I will answer only in the presence of my attorney."

The traditional formula . . . His face was bloodless. He faltered and stumbled as he tried to get up. Maigret had to bring him a glass of water.

THE AUTOPSY on Joséphine Croizier revealed that her heart was in excellent condition, and that she had been clumsily killed, first by attempted strangulation with a corset lace, then, doubtless because she was still struggling, by two knife wounds.

"I am compelled to congratulate you, Inspector," the prosecutor admitted with a glacial smile. "You are indeed the star performer that you are said to be. Nevertheless, I must confess to you that your methods, in a small city, are perilous."

"Which means I won't last long at Caen?"

"It is indeed true that——"

"Thanks."

"But——"

"I haven't been too happy here myself. My wife's waiting for me in Paris. All I hope is that your Caen jury won't be so impressed by the luxurious mansion of that blackguard Philippe that they'll forget to ask for the death penalty."

Deliberately Maigret struck a match, held it to his pipe, breathed in deeply, and launched a vast cloud of smoke into the sacrosanct office of the prosecutor of Caen.

The Most Obstinate Man in Paris

IN ALL THE ANNALS of the Paris Police no one had ever posed so long or so assiduously for a *portrait parlé*. For hours on end—sixteen, to be exact—he seemed so stubbornly intent on attracting attention that Inspector Janvier himself came in to look him over at close range. Yet when it was necessary to detail his description, the outlines were blurred and inexact. And some of the dozen witnesses, none of them regularly given to flights of imagination, were sure that the stranger's ostentation was nothing less than a skillful trick.

It all happened on May 3—a warm, sunny day with the special feel of a Parisian spring in the air. The chestnut trees of Boulevard Saint Germain were in full bloom and their delicate, faintly sweet fragrance drifted into the cool interior of the café from morning till night.

As he did every day, Joseph opened the doors of the café at eight in the morning. He was in vest and shirt sleeves. The sawdust he had scattered on the floor the night before at closing time was still there and the chairs were piled high on the marble-topped tables. For the Café des Ministères, at the corner of Boulevard Saint Germain and Rue des Saints Pères, was one of the rare old-fashioned cafés still left in Paris. It had resisted the influx of the hurried drinkers who had only time for a quick one. And it had resisted the rage of gilt fixtures, indirect lighting, mirrored pillars, and flimsy plastic taborets.

It was a café of regulars, where every customer had his own table in his own corner and his own cards or chess set. Joseph the waiter knew them all by name—most of them bureau chiefs and government clerks from neighboring ministries.

Joseph himself was something of a personage in his own right. He had been a waiter for thirty years and it was difficult to imagine him wearing street clothes. Most of his regular customers would probably not recognize him if they met him on the street or in the suburbs where he had built himself a little house.

Eight o'clock was the hour of cleaning up. The double door was wide open on Boulevard Saint Germain. There was sunshine on the sidewalk, but inside the café there was only cool, bluish shadow. Joseph smoked as he went about the ritual of getting ready for the day's business. It was his only cigarette of the day. First he lit the gas under the coffee boiler, then polished the nickel until it shone like a mirror. Next he put the bottles on the shelves behind the bar, the apéritifs first, then the other liquors. After that he swept up the sawdust and finally he set the chairs around the tables.

The man arrived at exactly ten minutes past eight. Joseph was busy at the coffee boiler and did not see him come in, a fact he afterward regretted. Had the man rushed in furtively like someone being pursued? And why had he chosen the Café des Ministères, when the bar across the street was already bustling with customers drinking their morning coffee and eating *croissants* and rolls?

As Joseph later described it: "I turned around and saw somebody already inside—a man wearing a gray hat and carrying a small suitcase."

The café was really open without being open. It was open because the doors were not closed, but nobody ever came in at this hour. The water was barely warm in the coffee machine and some of the chairs were still piled on the tables.

"I won't be able to serve you for at least half an hour," Joseph said.

He thought that settled matters, but the man merely lifted a chair from a table and sat down, still holding tight to his traveling bag.

"It really doesn't matter," said the stranger calmly, with the air of a man who is not easily dissuaded.

His tone was enough to put the waiter in bad humor. Joseph was like a housewife who hates to have people around at cleaning time. He had a right to be alone while he was doing his housework. He grumbled:

"You'll have a long wait for your coffee."

He continued his daily routine until nine o'clock, favoring the stranger with an occasional glance. Ten times, twenty times, he passed very close to the man, brushed against him, even jostled him a few times while he was sweeping up the sawdust and taking down the remainder of the chairs.

At a few minutes past nine he reluctantly brought the man a cup of scalding coffee, a small pitcher of milk, and two lumps of sugar on a saucer.

"Don't you have any *croissants?*"

"The place across the street has *croissants.*"

"It doesn't matter," the stranger said.

It was a curious thing, but this man who must know that he was in the way, who must know that he was in the wrong café at the wrong time, had a certain humility about him that made him rather likable. And there were other things Joseph noted with appreciation. During a whole hour the man did not take a newspaper from his pocket, nor did he ask for a paper, nor did he consult the directory or the telephone book. Nor did he try to engage the waiter in conversation. And that was not all: he did not smoke, he did not cross and uncross his legs, he did not fidget. He merely sat.

Not many people could sit in a café for an hour without moving, without looking at the time every few minutes, without showing their impatience in one way or another. If this man was waiting for someone, he was certainly waiting with extraordinary equanimity.

At precisely ten o'clock Joseph finished his housework. The man was still there. Another curious detail struck Joseph: the stranger had not taken a chair by the window, but sat at the rear of the café near the mahogany stairway that led down to the washrooms. Joseph would be going downstairs soon himself to spruce up a little, but first he cranked down the orange-colored awning, which gave a faint tint to the shadows inside.

Before going downstairs the waiter jingled a few coins in his vest pocket, hoping that the man would take the hint, pay his bill, and leave. The man did nothing of the kind. Joseph left him sitting alone as he went down to change his starched collar and dickey, comb his hair, and put on his worn alpaca jacket. When he came back, the man was still there, still gazing into his empty coffee cup.

Mademoiselle Berthe, the cashier, had come in and was sitting at her desk, taking things out of her handbag. Joseph winked at her. The cashier winked back and started arranging the brass checks in regular piles. She was plump, soft, pink, and placid, and her hair was bleached. When she had finished with the checks, she looked down at the stranger from her thronelike perch.

"He gave me the impression of being a very gentle, very respectable person," she said later. "And I could have wagered that he dyed his mustache, like the Colonel."

It was true that the blue-black tint of the man's little mustache suggested hair dye, just as the turned-up ends suggested the curling iron and wax.

Another part of the daily routine was the delivery of the ice. A giant with a piece of sacking on his shoulder carried in the opaline blocks, dripping a limpid trail as he put them away in the ice chest. He, too, noticed the solitary customer.

"He made me think of a sea lion," he said later.

Why a sea lion? The iceman couldn't say exactly.

As for Joseph, he kept strictly to his timetable. It was now time to remove yesterday's newspapers from their long-handled binders and to replace them with today's editions.

"Could I trouble you to pass me one of those?"

Well, well! The customer spoke at last—timidly, softly, but he spoke.

"Which paper do you want? *Le Temps? Le Figaro? Les Débats?*"

"It really doesn't matter."

That was another thing that made Joseph think that the man was not a Parisian. He was not a foreigner either, for he had no accent. Probably just off the train from the provinces. And yet there was no railway station in the immediate vicinity. Why would a man come halfway across Paris to sit in a strange café? And it was a strange café, because Joseph, who had a memory for faces, was certain that he had never seen the man before. Strangers who entered the Café des Ministères by chance knew at once that they did not belong there and promptly went away.

Eleven o'clock—the hour of the boss's arrival. Monsieur Monnet came downstairs from his apartment, freshly shaven, his cheeks aglow, his gray hair neatly slicked down, his perennial patent-leather shoes gleaming below his gray trousers. He could have retired from business long ago. He had bought a provincial café for each of his children, but he himself could live no other place in the world than this corner of Boulevard Saint Germain, where all his customers were his friends.

"Everything all right, Joseph?"

The boss had spotted the stranger and his coffee cup immediately. His eyes asked questions. Behind the counter Joseph whispered, "He's been here since eight this morning."

Monsieur Monnet walked back and forth in front of the stranger, rubbing his hands as if to invite conversation. Monsieur Monnet was used to talking to his customers. He played cards and dominoes with them. He knew their family troubles, their office gossip. But the stranger did not open his mouth.

"The man appeared very tired, like someone who had spent a sleepless night in a train," the boss said later.

And very much later Inspector Maigret asked the three of them, Joseph, Mademoiselle Berthe, and Monsieur Monnet, "Did he seem to be watching for somebody in the street?"

Their answers were different.

"No," said Monsieur Monnet.

"I got the impression he was waiting for a woman," said the cashier.

"Several times I caught him looking toward the bar across the street," said Joseph, "but each time he lowered his eyes almost immediately."

At twenty past eleven the stranger ordered a small bottle of Vichy. Several of Joseph's customers drank mineral water, and for reasons Joseph knew. Monsieur Blanc, for instance, of the War Ministry, was on a strict diet. Joseph noted that the stranger neither drank nor smoked, which was most unusual.

For the next two hours he lost track of the man, for the regulars had begun to swarm in for their before-lunch apéritifs. Joseph knew in advance what each would drink and to which tables he should bring playing cards.

"*Garçon!*"

It was past one. The stranger was still there. His suitcase had been pushed under the red-plush banquette. Joseph pretended that he thought the man was asking for the check, and he made his calculation half aloud.

"Eight francs fifty," he announced.

"Could you serve me a sandwich?"

"I'm sorry. We have none."

"Haven't you any rolls, either?"

"We don't serve any food here."

Which was both true and false. Sometimes in the evening a bridge player who had missed his dinner could get a ham sandwich, but it was not usual.

The man shook his head and murmured, "It really doesn't matter."

This time Joseph thought that the man's lips trembled slightly. He was struck by the resigned, sorrowful expression on the stranger's face.

"Could I serve you something?"

"Another coffee, please, with plenty of milk."

The man was hungry and the milk would be a little nourishment. He did not ask for other newspapers. He had had time to read the first one from first line to last, including the classified ads.

The Colonel arrived and was distinctly unhappy because there was someone seated at his table. The colonel was afraid of the slightest draft—spring drafts were the most treacherous of all—and always sat far back in the café.

Armand, the second waiter—he had been a waiter only three years and would never look like a real *garçon de café* if he remained a waiter all his life—came on duty at one-thirty. Joseph immediately went behind the glass partition to eat the lunch brought down from the second floor.

Why did Armand think that the stranger might have been a rug seller or a peanut vendor?

"He gave me the feeling of not being frank and open," said Armand later. "I didn't like the way he looked at you from under his eyelids. There was something oily, something too sweet in his face. If I had my way I'd have told him he was in the wrong pew and thrown him out on his ear."

Others noticed the man, particularly those who came back in the evening and found him sitting in exactly the same place.

True, all these witnesses were amateurs, but the professional who was to come upon the scene later was just as vague and full of contradictions.

For the first ten years of his career Joseph had been a waiter at the Brasserie Dauphine, a few steps from the Quai des Orfèvres, which was frequented by most of the inspectors and detectives of the Police Judiciaire. He had become a close friend of Inspector Janvier, one of Maigret's best men, and in time married Janvier's sister-in-law.

At three o'clock in the afternoon, seeing the man still in the same place, Joseph began to get really irritated. He formulated a hypothesis, to wit, that if this fellow stubbornly clung to his banquette it was not for love of the atmosphere inside the Café des Ministères but for fear of what lay outside. When he got off the train, Joseph reasoned, the man must have felt that he was being followed, and had come to the café to avoid the police. So Joseph telephoned the Quai des Orfèvres and asked for Inspector Janvier.

"I've got a funny customer here who's been sitting in his corner since eight this morning and who seems determined not to budge," he said. "He hasn't eaten anything all day. Don't you think you ought to come over and take a look at him?"

The meticulous Janvier packed up a collection of the latest "Wanted" notices and headed for Boulevard Saint Germain. By a curious chance, at the very moment he stepped into the Café des Ministères, the place was empty.

"Flown the coop?" he asked Joseph.

The waiter pointed to the basement stairs. "Gone to telephone."

What a pity! A few minutes sooner and Janvier could have had the call monitored. As it was, the inspector sat down and ordered a calvados.

The stranger came back to his table, still calm, perhaps a trifle worried, but certainly not nervous. Joseph, who was getting to know the man, thought him rather relaxed.

For the next twenty minutes Janvier scrutinized the stranger from head to foot. He had plenty of time to compare the plump, rather vague features with the photos of the most-wanted criminals. Then he shrugged.

"He's not on our lists," Janvier told Joseph. "He looks to me like some poor guy who's been stood up by a woman. He's probably an insurance agent or something of the sort." He chuckled. "I wouldn't be surprised if he turned out to be a coffin salesman. Anyhow, I don't see that I have any right to pick him up. There's no law against a man going without lunch, if he wants to, or sitting all day in a café, as long as he pays his tab."

After chatting with Joseph a while longer Janvier returned to the Quai des Orfèvres for an appointment with Maigret. The two inspectors were so engrossed in a gambling case that Janvier forgot even to mention to Maigret the man of Boulevard Saint Germain.

The dying rays of the sun slanted so low that they slid under the awnings of the Café des Ministères. At five o'clock three tables were taken by *belote* players. Monsieur Monnet himself took a hand at a table just opposite the stranger. From time to time he glanced at the man, who still sat motionless.

By six o'clock the café was jammed. Joseph and Armand hurried from table to table, their trays loaded with bottles and glasses. The aroma of Pernod soon overpowered the delicate scent of the blossoming chestnut trees on the boulevard.

Each of the two waiters, during the rush hour, had his own tables. The man was sitting at a table in Armand's section. Not only was Armand less observant than his colleague, but he occasionally slipped behind the counter to toss off a glass of white wine. It was understandable, therefore, that the events of the evening may have seemed somewhat blurred to him.

All he could say for sure was that a woman finally came in.

"She was a brunette, well dressed, respectable-looking, not at all one of these women who sometimes drop into a café and try to strike up a conversation with strangers."

She was, according to Armand, a woman who would wait in a public place only because she had a date with her husband.

There were several vacant tables, but she sat down at the table next to the man.

"I'm sure they didn't speak to one another," Armand said later. "She ordered a glass of port. I think I remember that besides her handbag—a brown or black leather bag—she was carrying a small package in her hand. I noticed it on the table when she ordered the port. It was tied up in paper. But when I brought her order, the package was no longer on the table. She had probably put it on the banquette beside her."

Too bad that Joseph did not see the woman more clearly.

Mademoiselle Berthe saw her all right, from her high-perched desk.

"Rather nicely turned out," the cashier said later. "She wore a blue tailored suit, a white blouse, and almost no make-up. I don't know why I say this, but I don't think she was a married woman."

There was a constant flow of customers in and out of the café until eight o'clock, the dinner hour. Then the vacant tables began to be more numerous. At nine o'clock only six other tables were occupied, two by bridge players who never missed a daily session, and four by chess players.

"One thing is certain," Joseph said later, "the man knew bridge. And chess, too. I'd say he was a demon at both. I could tell by the way he was watching the games around him."

So he was not at all preoccupied? Or was Joseph mistaken?

At ten o'clock only three other tables were occupied. The men from the ministries went to bed early. At half-past ten Armand went home. His wife was expecting a baby and he had arranged with the boss to leave early.

The man was still there, still sitting quietly.

Since ten minutes past eight that morning he had drunk three cups of coffee, a split of Vichy, and a bottle of lemon pop— nothing stronger. He had not smoked. He had read *Le Temps* during the morning and late in the afternoon he had bought an evening paper from a news vendor who passed through the café.

At eleven o'clock Joseph started piling the chairs on the tables, as he did every evening, although two tables were still occupied. He also scattered the sawdust on the floor, as usual.

A little later one game broke up. Monsieur Monnet shook hands with his partners, one of whom was the colonel, went to the cashier's desk for the little canvas bag into which Mademoiselle Berthe had stuffed the sheaves of bank notes and the small change, and climbed the stairs to his apartment.

Before leaving he glanced once more at the obstinate customer who had been a topic of general conversation that evening and said to Joseph:

"If he makes any trouble, ring me."

There was a push button behind the bar that set off an alarm in Monsieur Monnet's private apartment.

And that was the whole story. When Maigret started his investigation next day, there was little more to be learned.

Mademoiselle Berthe had left at ten minutes to eleven to catch the last bus for Epinay. She, too, had looked at the stranger one final time before leaving.

"I can't say that he was nervous, exactly, but he wasn't exactly calm either. If I'd met him in the street, for instance, he would have scared me, if you know what I mean. And if he'd got off the bus at my stop in Epinay, I wouldn't have dared walk home alone."

"Why?"

"Well, he had one of those inward looks."

"What do you mean by that?"

"He didn't pay attention to anything that was going on around him."

"Were the shutters of the café closed?"

"No. Joseph doesn't lower them until the last minute."

"From your desk you can see the street corner and the bar across the street. Did you notice any suspicious movements in either place? Did you see anyone who might have been watching for him, waiting for him?"

"I wouldn't have noticed. As quiet as it is on Boulevard Saint

Germain side, there's quite a bit of traffic on Rue des Saints Pères. And there's always people coming in and going out of the bar across the street."

"You didn't notice anyone outside this café when you left to go home?"

"Nobody. No, wait. There was a police officer at the corner."

The statement was confirmed by the district police station. Unfortunately the policeman was to leave his post a few minutes later.

Only two other tables were now taken, one by a couple who had dropped in for a drink after the movies, a doctor and his wife who lived a few doors down and often had a nightcap on their way home. They were considered regulars of the Café des Ministères. They had paid their check and were leaving.

The doctor said, "We were sitting just opposite him, and I observed that he was not a well man."

"In your opinion, Doctor, what was wrong with him?"

"His liver, no doubt about it."

"How old would you say he was?"

"It's hard to say. I'm sorry now that I didn't pay more careful attention. In my opinion he was one of those men who look older than their age. Some people would say he was forty-five or even more because of the dyed mustache."

"He did dye his mustache, then? You're sure of that?"

"I think he did. However, I've known patients of thirty-five with the same flabby, colorless flesh, the same lifeless air. . . ."

"Don't you think the fact that he had nothing to eat all day may have given him his lifeless air?"

"Possibly. Nevertheless, that would not change my diagnosis. The man had a bad stomach, a bad liver, and, I may add, a defective intestinal tract."

The bridge game at the last occupied table—the last except the stranger's—went on and on. Every time game and rubber seemed on the point of ending the contest, the declarer failed to make his bid. At last a contract of five clubs, doubled and redoubled, was miraculously made, thanks to the nervous error of a tired player who unintentionally established the dummy's long side suit.

It was ten minutes before midnight when Joseph piled the last chairs on a table and announced: "We're closing, *messieurs*."

The stranger did not move while the bridge players were settling their bill, and Joseph would have admitted that at that moment he was frightened. He was on the point of asking the four regulars to wait while he put the man out, but somehow he didn't dare. The regulars filed out, still talking about the last hand. They continued arguing for a moment on the street corner and then separated.

"Eighteen francs seventy-five," Joseph said, a shade too loudly. He was now alone with the stranger. He had already extinguished half the lights.

"I had my eye on an empty siphon of seltzer left over on the corner of the bar," he confessed to Maigret afterward. "One move and I would have bashed his head in."

"Did you put the siphon bottle there for that express purpose?"

Obviously he had. Sixteen hours spent with the enigmatic stranger had put Joseph's nerves on edge. The man had become a personal enemy, almost. Little by little Joseph had practically convinced himself that the man was there on the waiter's account exclusively, that he was waiting only for a propitious moment, a moment when they would be alone, to attack and rob him.

And yet Joseph made one mistake. While the man was fumbling in his pockets for change, still seated at his table, the waiter had gone out to crank down the iron shutters. He was afraid of missing his bus. True, the door was still wide open and there were still pedestrians on the boulevard, taking advantage of the midnight coolness.

"Here you are, *garçon*."

Twenty-one francs! Two francs twenty-five tip for a whole day! Joseph was furious. Only his professional composure of thirty years kept him from throwing the change back on the table.

"And maybe you were a little afraid of him, too?" Inspector Maigret suggested.

"I really don't know. Anyhow, I was in a hurry to be rid of him. In all my life I've never been infuriated by a customer like that. If I'd only foreseen that morning that he was going to stay all day!"

"Where were you at the exact moment he left the café?"

"Let me see . . . First I had to remind him that he had a suitcase under the banquette. He was going off without it."

"Did he seem annoyed that you reminded him of it?"

"No."

"Did he seem relieved?"

"He didn't act pleased or displeased. Indifferent, I would say. If I was looking for a cool customer, this was a cool customer. I've seen all kinds and shapes in the thirty years I've been a waiter, but I've never seen one who could sit behind a marble-topped table for sixteen hours straight without getting ants in his pants."

"And where were you standing?"

"Near the cashier's desk. I was ringing up the eighteen francs seventy-five. You've noticed there are two entrances here—the big double door that opens on the boulevard and the little one on Rue des Saints Pères. When he headed for the side door, I was going to call him back and show him the main entrance, but then I thought, *What's the difference? It's all the same to me.* I was through for the night, except to change my clothes and lock up."

"In what hand was he carrying his suitcase?"

"I didn't notice."

"And I suppose you didn't notice either if he had one hand in his pocket?"

"I don't know. He wasn't wearing a topcoat. I didn't actually see him go out on account of the chairs piled on the tables. They cut off my view."

"You kept standing in the same place?"

"Yes, right here. I was taking the ticket out of the cash register with one hand, and with the other I was fishing in my pocket for the last of the day's brass checks. Then I heard an explosion—like a car backfiring. Only I knew right away it wasn't a car. I said to myself, 'Well, well! So he got it after all!'

"You think very fast at a time like that. You have to in my line of business. I've seen some pretty tough brawls in my life. I'm always amazed at how fast a man thinks.

"I was mad at myself. After all, he was just a poor guy who had hid out here because he knew he'd get knocked off the minute he stuck his nose outside. So I was sorry for him. He didn't eat anything all day, so maybe he didn't have the money to call a taxi and make a getaway before he got ambushed."

"Did you rush right out to help him?"

"Well, as a matter of fact . . ." Joseph was embarrassed. "I think I probably hesitated a moment. I've got a wife and three children, you know. So first I pushed the button that rings in the boss's bedroom. Then I heard voices outside, and the sound of people running in the street. I heard a woman say, 'You stay out of this, Gaston.' Then I heard a police whistle.

"I went out. I saw three people on Rue des Saints Pères, several yards from the door."

"Eight yards," said Inspector Maigret, consulting the police report.

"Possibly. I didn't measure. A man was lying in the street and another man was stooping over him. I found out afterward it was a doctor who was on his way home from the movies and who just happens to be a customer of ours. We have quite a few doctors among our regulars.

"The doctor stood up and said, 'He's had it. The bullet entered the back of his neck and came out through the left eye.'

"Then the police officer arrived and I knew I'd be questioned. Believe it or not, I just couldn't look at the ground. That business about the left eye made me sick to my stomach. I didn't want to look at my customer in that shape, with his eye shot out. I told myself that it was partly my fault, that perhaps I should have—— But after all, what could I have done?

"I can still hear the voice of the police officer, standing there with his notebook in his hand, asking: 'Doesn't anybody know this man?' And I answered automatically, 'I do. At least I think I——'

"Finally I forced myself to bend down and look. I swear to you, Monsieur Maigret—and you know me well enough, what with all the thousands of glasses of beer and calvados I used to serve you over at the Brasserie Dauphine, Inspector, to understand I'm not given to exaggerating—I swear to you I never had such a shock in my life.

"*It was not the man!* It was not the stranger who had sat all day in the café.

"It was somebody I didn't know, somebody I never saw before —a tall, skinny man in a raincoat. On a fine spring day, a night warm enough to sleep under the stars, and he was wearing a tan raincoat.

"I felt better. Maybe it's silly, but I was glad it wasn't our customer. If my customer had been the victim instead of the murderer, I would have felt guilty about it all my life. You see, since early morning I felt there was something not quite right about my man. I would have put my hand in the fire, that he was a wrong one. It wasn't for nothing that I phoned Janvier. Only Janvier, even if he is practically my brother-in-law, always does everything according to the rules. When I called him, why didn't he ask to see the man's identity papers? They would have told him something, certainly. A decent law-abiding citizen doesn't sit all day in a café and then go out and shoot somebody on the sidewalk at midnight.

"Because you'll note that he didn't loiter after the shot was fired. Nobody saw him. If he wasn't the one that pulled the trigger, he would have stayed right there. He couldn't have walked more than a dozen steps by the time I heard the gun go off.

"The only thing I don't understand is about this woman—the one that ordered a glass of port from Armand. How does she fit into this? Because there's no doubt she had something to do with this man. We don't get many unescorted women in our café—it's not that kind of a place."

"I thought," Inspector Maigret objected, "that the man and the woman did not speak to each other."

"Did they have to speak? Didn't she have a little package in her hand when she came in? Armand saw it, and Armand is not a liar. He saw it on the table and then he saw it wasn't on the table any more and he supposed she'd put it on the banquette. And when this lady left, Mademoiselle Berthe watched her go out because she was admiring her handbag and wishing she had one like it. Now Mademoiselle Berthe didn't notice that she was carrying a package then, and you must admit that women do notice such things.

"You can say what you like, but I still think I spent the whole day with a murderer. And I think I got off very lucky."

DAWN BROUGHT one of those perfect spring days such as Paris manages to produce about every third year, a day meant for nothing more strenuous than eating a sherbet or remembering the carefree days of childhood. Everything was good, light, heady, and of rare quality: the limpid blue of the sky, the fleecy whiteness of the few clouds, the softness of the breeze that kissed your cheek as you turned a corner and that rustled the chestnut trees just enough to make you raise your eyes to admire the clusters of sweet flowers. A cat on a window sill, a dog stretched out on the sidewalk, a shoemaker in his leather apron leaning in his doorway for a breath of air, an ordinary green and yellow bus rumbling by—they were all precious that day, all designed to instill gaiety into the soul.

That is probably why Inspector Maigret has always kept such a delightful memory of the corner of Boulevard Saint Germain and Rue des Saints Pères. It is also the reason he was later to stop frequently at a certain café for a spot of shade and a glass of beer.

Unfortunately the beer never tasted quite the same after that day.

The case he was investigating was destined to become famous, not because of the inexplicable obstinacy of the stranger in the Café des Ministères, or of the midnight shooting, but because of the strange motive for the crime.

At eight the next morning Inspector Maigret was at his desk in the Quai des Orfèvres, all of his windows open on the blue and gold panorama of the Seine. He smoked his pipe with small, gluttonous puffs as he skimmed through the reports—and thus made his first contact with the man of the Café des Ministères and with the death on Rue des Saints Pères.

The police of the district commissariat had put in a good night's work. Dr. Paul, the medical examiner, had finished his autopsy by six in the morning. The bullet and the empty shell case, which had both been found on the sidewalk, had already been submitted to Gastinne-Renette, the ballistics expert, and a report was expected shortly.

The dead man's clothes, together with the contents of his pockets and several photographs of the scene made by Identification, were on Maigret's desk. Maigret picked up his phone.

"Would you step into my office, Janvier? According to the report, you seem to be somewhat involved in this case."

And so on that beautiful spring day Maigret and Janvier were once again teammates.

Maigret studied the clothing while he waited. The suit was of good quality and less worn than it seemed. It was the suit of a man who lived alone, without a woman to brush it off occasionally or to make him send it to the cleaners before it looked as though he had slept in it—which perhaps he had. The shirt was new and had not yet been to the laundry, but it had been worn for at least a week. The socks looked no better.

There were no papers in the pockets, no letters, no clues to the man's identity. The usual miscellany had some unusual additions: a corkscrew; a pocketknife with numerous blades; a dirty handkerchief; a button off his jacket; a single key; a well-caked pipe and a tobacco pouch; a wallet containing two thousand three hundred and fifty francs and a snapshot of half a dozen bare-bosomed native girls standing in front of an African straw hut; a piece of string; and a third-class railway ticket from Juvisy to Paris, bearing the date of the previous day. And finally there was a toy printing set, the kind with which children could fit rubber letters into a small wooden frame and make their own rubber stamps.

The rubber letters in the frame formed the words:

I'LL GET YOU YET.

The medical examiner's report contained several interesting details. The shot had been fired from behind at a distance of not more than ten feet. Death had been instantaneous. The dead man had numerous scars. The ones on his feet were obviously caused by chigoes, African jiggers that burrow under the skin and have to be dug out with the point of a knife. His liver was in pitiful condition, a real drunkard's liver. And finally the man killed on Rue des Saints Pères had been suffering from a bad case of malaria.

"Here you are!" Maigret reached for his hat. "Let's go, Janvier, old man."

They walked to the Café des Ministères. Through the window they could see Joseph busy with his morning housework. But curiously enough Maigret was more interested in the café across the street.

The two cafés were opposite in more ways than geographically. Joseph's domain was old-fashioned and quiet. The bar on the opposite corner—the sign read: "Chez Léon"—was aggressively and vulgarly modern. At the long bar two waiters in shirt sleeves worked busily behind pyramids of *croissants*, sandwiches, and hard-boiled eggs. Now they were serving little but coffee and white wine. Later it would be red wine and anise-flavored apéritifs.

At the far end of the bar the proprietor and his wife alternated at the tobacco counter. Beyond was the back room, garish with its red and gold pillars, its one-legged tables in rainbow plastic, and its chairs covered with goffered plush of an incredible red hue.

All the bay windows opened on the street and crowds swarmed in and out of the Chez Léon from morning to night—masons in powdery smocks, clerks and typists, delivery boys rushing in for quick ones before reclaiming their parked tricycle carriers; people in a hurry, people looking for a phone, and, most of all, people who were thirsty.

"One up! . . . Two Beaujolais! . . . Three bocks!"

The cast register played a continuous tune. The waiters and barmen sweated as they worked, sometimes mopping their brows with bar towels. Dirty glasses, dipped in murky water, did not even have time to dry before they were refilled with red or white wine.

"Two dry whites," Maigret ordered. He loved the din and tumult of the morning rush. And he liked the rascally aftertaste of the white wine he never found anywhere but in bistros of this sort.

"Tell me, *garçon*, do you remember this man?"

Identification had done a good job. Photographing a dead man may be an ignoble way of earning a living, but it is an essential and delicate art. The inexpert result is often hard to recognize, especially if the face has been damaged. So the gentlemen from Identification first touch up the corpse, then retouch the negative so that the subject looks almost alive.

"That's him, all right. Isn't it, Louis?"

The other waiter looked over his partner's shoulder.

"Sure, that's the guy who bothered hell out of us all day yesterday. How could we forget him?"

"Do you remember what time he first came in?"

"Well, that's hard to say. He's not a regular. But I remember around ten o'clock this guy was all steamed up about something. He couldn't sit still. He came to the bar and asked for a slug of white. He gulped it down, paid, and went out. Ten minutes later he was back, sitting at a table, yelling for another slug of white."

"So he was in here all day?"

"I think so. Anyhow I saw him at least ten or fifteen times. He kept getting more and more jittery. He had a funny way of looking at you, and his hands trembled when he handed you the money. Like an old woman's. Didn't he break a glass on you, Louis?"

"He did. And he insisted on picking all the pieces out of the sawdust himself. He'd say, 'It's white glass. That's good luck. And do I need good luck, specially today. You ever been in the Gabon, lad?' he'd keep asking."

"He talked to me about the Gabon, too," said the other waiter. "He was eating hard-boiled eggs. He'd eaten twelve or thirteen in a row, and I thought he was going to bust, particularly as he'd had quite a lot to drink. So he said to me, 'Don't be afraid, lad. One time in the Gabon I made a bet I could swallow three dozen, with thirty-six beers along with the eggs, and I won.' "

"Did he seem preoccupied?" Maigret asked.

"Depends on what you mean by that. He kept going out and coming back. I thought he was waiting for somebody. Sometimes I caught him laughing all by himself, like he'd been telling himself jokes. And once he cornered an old man who comes in every afternoon for two-three slugs of red, a nice old man. He grabbed the old man's lapels and talked his ear off for an hour."

"Did you know he was armed?"

"How could I know that?"

"Because a man of his type is apt to show off his revolver in a bar."

It was indeed a revolver. The police had found it on the sidewalk beside the body. It was a large-caliber gun, loaded but unfired.

"Let's have more of that white wine."

Maigret was in such high spirits that he could not resist the solicitations of a barefooted flower girl who came in at that moment. She was a skinny, dirty little elf with the most beautiful eyes in the world. Impulsively he bought a bouquet of violets which he then did not know what to do with, so he stuffed it into his coat pocket.

It must be said that this was a day for white wine. A little later Maigret and Janvier crossed the street and entered the savory gloom of the Café des Ministères. Joseph rushed to meet them.

Here they tried to straighten out the blurred portrait of the man with the little suitcase and the blue-black mustache. Or perhaps "blurred" is not the word. The picture was rather one in which either the subject or the camera had moved, or had been developed from a film with double or triple exposure.

No two descriptions matched. Everyone saw the stranger in a different light. And now there was even one witness—the colonel —who swore that the minute he saw the man he was sure he was up to no good.

Some remembered the man as terribly nervous, others as amazingly calm. Maigret listened to them all, nodding, stuffing his pipe with a meticulous forefinger, lighting it with great care, smoking with little puffs, narrowing his eyes like a man enjoying a wonderful day—a day on which heaven, in a fit of good humor, had decided to be generous to all mankind.

"About this woman——"

"You mean the girl?"

Joseph, who had caught only a glimpse of her, was convinced it was a girl—a pretty girl, distinguished and obviously of good family. He was sure that she did not work for a living. He imagined her in comfortable bourgeois surroundings, baking pastry or making genteel desserts for her family.

Mademoiselle Berthe, on the other hand, had doubts.

"I for one," the cashier said, "would hesitate to give her absolution without confession. However, I do admit that she seemed a lot more decent than the man."

There were moments when Maigret wanted to yawn and

stretch himself, as though he were in the country, lying in the sun. That morning he found life enchanting at the corner of Boulevard Saint Germain and Rue des Saints Pères. He was fascinated by the bus stopping and starting, by the passengers climbing aboard, by the ritual gesture of the conductor reaching for the bell. And what could be more lovely than the moving shadow patterns on the sidewalk, the leafy tapestry of the chestnut trees?

"I'll bet he hasn't gone very far," Maigret grumbled to Janvier, who was still annoyed at not being able to give a more exact description of the man, after having looked him right in the face.

The two detectives left the café and paused a moment at the curb, staring at the bar across the street. Two men, two bars, one for each. It would appear that Fate had planted each man in his proper atmosphere: in one the calm man with the little mustache, the man who could sit all day without moving, who could live on coffee and soda, who did not even protest when Joseph told him that there was nothing to eat. And across the street, in the noise and confusion of little people, of the crowd of secretaries and workmen and delivery boys, in the mad rush of white wine and hard-boiled eggs, the man who was too excited to wait, who popped in and out, buttonholing people to talk to them of the Gabon.

"I'll bet that there's a third café," said Maigret, staring across the boulevard.

In that he was wrong. True, there was across the street a window that commanded a view of both corners and a window that obviously belonged to a public place of some kind. But it was neither bar nor café. It was a restaurant called A l'Escargot.

The restaurant consisted of one long, low-ceilinged room that was reached by two steps down from the street level. It was obviously a restaurant with a regular clientele, for along the wall there was a row of pigeonholes in which the diners could leave their napkins. The pleasant garlicky aroma of good cooking permeated the place. It was the proprietress herself who emerged from the kitchen to greet them.

"What is it, *messieurs?*"

Maigret identified himself. He then said, "I'd like to know if you had a customer here last night who lingered over his dinner much longer than is usual in your restaurant."

The woman hesitated. There was no one in the dining room. The tables were already set for lunch. At each place there were tiny decanters of red and white wine.

"I spend most of my time in the kitchen," she said. "My husband would know. He's usually at the cash desk, but he's out right now buying fruit. Our waiter, François, doesn't come on until eleven, but he won't be long now. May I serve you something while you're waiting? We have a little Corsican wine you might like. My husband has it shipped direct."

Everybody was charming this fine spring day. The little Corsican wine was charming too. And the low-ceilinged dining room where the two detectives waited for François was delightful. They watched the parade of pedestrians and the two cafés across the boulevard.

"You have an idea, Chief?"

"I've got several. But which is the right one, that's the question."

François arrived. He was a white-thatched old man who would never be taken for anything but a restaurant waiter. He backed halfway into a closet to change his clothes.

"Tell me, waiter. Do you remember a diner last night who acted rather strangely? A girl with dark hair?"

"A lady," François corrected. "Anyhow, I noticed she wore a wedding ring, a red-gold band. I noticed it because my wife and I wear red-gold wedding rings too. Look."

"Was she young?"

"I'd say about thirty. Quite a proper person, well spoken, with almost no make-up."

"What time did she come in?"

"At quarter-past six, just as I finished setting the tables for dinner. Our regular clientele hardly ever gets here before seven. She seemed surprised by the empty room and started to turn around. 'Do you want dinner?' I asked, because sometimes people come in by mistake, thinking this is a café. 'Come in,' I said. 'I can serve you dinner in about fifteen minutes. Would you like something to drink while you're waiting?' And she ordered a glass of port."

Maigret and Janvier exchanged satisfied glances.

"She sat down near the window. I had to ask her to move because she was sitting at the table of the gentlemen from the Registry Office. They've been coming here regularly for ten years and they don't like to sit at any other table. . . . Actually, she had to wait nearly half an hour because the snails were not ready. She wasn't impatient, though. I brought her a newspaper, but she didn't read it. She just sat quietly and looked out the window."

Just like the man with the blue-black mustache. A calm man and a calm woman. And at the other corner a madcap with nerves as taut as violin strings. Only at this point in the drama it was the madcap who had the gun. It was the madcap who had a rubber stamp in his pocket with the threat: *"I'LL GET YOU YET."*

And it was the madcap who had died without firing his gun.

"A very gentle woman," François was saying. "I thought she must be somebody from the neighborhood who had forgotten her key and was waiting for her husband to come home. That happens oftener than people think, you know."

"Did she eat with good appetite?"

"Let me see . . . A dozen snails . . . Then some sweetbreads, some cheese and some strawberries and cream. I remember because those dishes all cost extra on the menu. She drank a small carafe of white wine and then a cup of coffee.

"She stayed quite late. That's what made me think she was waiting for somebody. She wasn't the last to leave, but there were only two other people here when she asked for her check. It must have been after ten o'clock. We usually close at ten-thirty."

"Do you know which direction she took when she left?"

"I hope you gentlemen don't mean any harm to this lady?" The old waiter seemed to have an affection for his one-night customer. "Good. So then I can tell you that when I left here myself at quarter to eleven, I was surprised to see her across the street, standing near a tree. Look, it was the second tree to the left of the lamppost."

"Was she still waiting for someone?"

"She must have been. She's not the sort you're thinking of. When she saw me, she turned her head away, as if she was embarrassed."

"Tell me, waiter, did she have a handbag?"

"Of course."

"Was it big? Small? Did you see her open it?"

"Just a moment . . . No, she didn't open it. She put it on the window sill next to her table. It was of dark leather, rectangular, fairly large. It had a big letter on it—an *M*, I think, in silver or some other metal."

"Well, Janvier, old man?"

"Well, Chief?"

If they drank many more of these little glasses here and there, they would end up this fine spring day by acting like a couple of schoolboys on vacation.

"Do you think she killed him?"

"We know he was killed from behind, at not more than ten feet."

"But the man in the Café des Ministères could have——"

"Just a moment, Janvier. Which of these two men was going to attack the other?"

"The dead man."

"Who was not yet dead, but who was certainly armed. So he was the menace, the ambusher. He was a threat to the other. Under these conditions, unless he was dead drunk by midnight, it is unlikely that the other could have surprised *him* and shot *him* from behind on emerging from the Café des Ministères, especially at such short range. On the other hand, the woman——"

"What do we do now?"

If Maigret followed his inclination, they would have loitered a while longer in the neighborhood. He liked the atmosphere. He would go back for another white wine with Joseph. Then back to the bar across the street. Sniff around. Drink a little more wine. Play different variations on the same theme: a man with a waxed mustache here; a man across the street, rotten with fever and alcohol; and finally a woman so respectable-looking that she had conquered the heart of old François, eating snails, sweetbreads, and strawberries and cream.

"I'll bet she's used to simple family cooking and eats out very rarely," said Maigret.

"Why do you say that, Chief?"

"The menu. She ordered three dishes that cost more than the regular dinner. People who eat out regularly don't do that, particularly two of the dishes you rarely get at home—snails and sweetbreads. The two don't go together. The fact that she ordered them indicates she is something of a gourmand."

"You think a woman about to commit murder gives much thought to what she's eating?"

"First of all, my dear Janvier, we know nothing that *proves* she was going to kill anyone last night."

"If she did kill him, she must have been armed. Right? I got the drift of your questions about the handbag. I was waiting for you to ask the waiter if he thought it might be heavy."

"Second," Maigret went on, ignoring the interruption, "even the most poignant tragedy will not make most human beings unaware of what they are eating. You must have seen it as clearly as I have. Somebody is dead. The house is upside down. The place is filled with tears and wailing. Life will never resume its normal rhythm. Then somebody comes in to fix dinner—an old aunt, a neighbor, a neighbor's maid. 'I couldn't swallow a mouthful,' the

widow swears. Everybody coaxes her. They make her sit down
to the table. The whole family abandons the corpse and sits down
with her. After a minute everybody is eating with gusto. And
the widow is asking for the salt and pepper because the ragout
needs seasoning . . . Let's go, my dear Janvier."

"Where to, Chief?"

"To Juvisy."

They really should have caught a suburban train at the Gare de
Lyon, but Maigret was horrified at the thought of ending a perfect spring day by fighting crowds of commuters at the ticket
windows and on the platforms, ending up either in a No Smoking
compartment or standing in the corridor. So, refusing to envisage
what the auditor at Police Judiciaire might say about his expense
account, Maigret hailed a taxi—an open car, almost brand-new
—and spread himself luxuriously on the cushions.

"Juvisy," he told the driver. "Drop us across from the railway
station."

He half closed his eyes and spent the journey in a delicious
trance, only the trail of smoke from his pipe indicating that he
was not asleep.

FOR A LONG TIME, whenever he was asked to tell the story of one
of his most famous cases, Inspector Maigret used to describe some
investigation in which his stubborn persistence, his intuition, and
his sense of human values literally forced the truth to the sur-
face.

Nowadays, however, the story he likes to tell is the case of the
two cafés on Boulevard Saint Germain, even though his own part
in it was a rather slim one. And when he finishes with a satisfied
smile that is almost a smacking of the lips, someone inevitably
asks, "But what is the true story?"

Maigret smiles even more and says, "It's up to you. Pick the
one you like best."

For on at least one point the whole truth was never discovered by Maigret or by anyone else.

It was half past twelve when the taxi dropped the two inspectors opposite the suburban railway station of Juvisy. The detectives first entered the Restaurant du Triage, an undistinguished oasis with a terrace surrounded by bay trees in green tubs. They exchanged questioning glances. Could they enter a café—especially today—without taking a drink? Maigret shrugged. In as much as they had devoted themselves so far to white wine, like the dead man of Rue des Saints Pères, they might as well continue.

Maigret produced his retouched photograph of the cadaver and showed it to the prize-fighter-looking man who was operating behind the zinc bar.

"Tell me, *patron*," he said, "do you recognize this face?"

The man behind the bar held the picture at arm's length and squinted at it, as if he were farsighted.

"Julie, come here a minute," he called. "Isn't this the bird from next door?"

His wife came in, wiping her hands on her blue denim apron. She took the photograph gingerly in her fingers.

"Why, sure it is!" she exclaimed. "But he has a funny expression in this picture, hasn't he?" Turning to Maigret, she added, "Probably stiff again. He's a great drinker. Just last night he kept us up past eleven o'clock, tossing them off."

"Last night?" Maigret was startled.

"No, wait a minute. It must have been the night before last. Yesterday I did my washing and last night I went to the movies."

"Can we have lunch here?"

"Sure you can have lunch. What do you want to eat? Veal fricandeau? Roast pork with lentils? And you can start with a good homemade pâté."

They ate outside on the terrace, next to the taxi driver they had asked to wait. From time to time the tavern keeper came out to talk to them.

"My neighbor next door can tell you a lot more than I can,"

he said. "He rents rooms. We don't. Your man has been staying
there for the last month or two. When it comes to drinking,
though, he drinks all over town. Why, just yesterday morning——"

"Are you sure it was yesterday?"

"Positive. I was just opening up at six-thirty when he came
in. He tossed off two or three glasses of white wine. 'To kill
the worms,' he said. Then all of a sudden he grabbed his raincoat and ran for the station. The Paris train was just leaving."

The tavern keeper knew nothing about the man except that he
drank a lot of wine, that he talked about the Gabon with or without the slightest provocation, that he was contemptuous of anyone
who had not lived in Africa, and that he bore a bitter grudge
against somebody. Who? The tavern keeper didn't know, but he
repeated a speech the man with the raincoat had once made:

"Some people think they are very clever, but they're not clever
enough. I'll get them in the end. Sure, anybody can be a skunk
at times, but there's a limit on how much of a skunk a man can be."

Half an hour later Janvier and Maigret were talking to the proprietor of the Hôtel du Chemin de Fer. It looked exactly
like the place next door except that there were no bay trees around
the terrace and the chairs were painted red, not green.

The proprietor had been behind the bar when they came in,
reading a newspaper aloud to his wife and his waiter. When
Maigret saw the likeness of the dead man on page one, he knew
that the first editions of the evening papers had reached Juvisy.
He himself had sent the photographs to the press.

"That your tenant?" Maigret asked.

The proprietor darted a suspicious glance. He put down the
paper.

"Yes. So?"

"Nothing. I just wanted to know if he was your tenant."

"Good riddance, in any case."

Maigret hesitated. They were going to have to drink something again and it was too soon after lunch to drink any more white wine.

"Calvados," he ordered. "Two."

"You from the police?"

"Yes."

"I thought so. Your face is familiar. So?"

"I'm asking you what you think of the murder."

"I would have thought that he was the one to shoot somebody else, not get shot himself. Although it wouldn't have surprised me if he'd got his face kicked in. He was impossible when he was drunk, and he was drunk every night."

"Do you have his registration blank?"

With great dignity, to show that he had nothing to hide, the proprietor went for his register, which he offered to Inspector Maigret with just a touch of contempt. The entry read:

> *Ernest Combarieu. Age 47. Born at Marsily, la Rochelle arrondissement (Charente-Maritime). Occupation: woodcutter. Coming from: Libreville, French Equatorial Africa.*

"I hear he stayed with you for six weeks."

"Six weeks too long."

"Didn't he pay his bill?"

"He paid regularly every week. But he was a lunatic—stark crazy. He used to stay in bed with the fever two or three days at a time, and he'd order rum sent up to cure him. He drank the rum right out of the bottle. Then he'd get up and make the rounds of every bistro in town. Sometimes he'd forget to come home, sometimes he'd wake us up at three o'clock in the morning to let him in. Sometimes I had to undress him and put him to bed. He used to vomit on the stairway carpet or on the rug in his room."

"Did he have any family here in town?"

Husband and wife looked at each other.

"He knew somebody here, that's certain. If it was a relative, our friend didn't like him, I can guarantee you that. He used to say to me, 'One of these days you're going to hear news about me and a scoundrel who everybody thinks is an honest man, but who is really a dirty hypocrite and the worst thief in the world.' "

"You never knew which man he was talking about?"

"All I know is that our tenant was unbearable and that when he was drunk he had the crazy habit of pulling out a big revolver, aiming across the room, and shouting, 'Bang! Bang!' Then he would burst out laughing and order another drink."

"You'll have a little drink with us, won't you?" said Maigret. "One more question. Do you know a gentleman in Juvisy who is medium height, plump but not fat, with a fine turned-up black mustache and who sometimes carries a small suitcase?"

The proprietor turned to his wife. "That mean anything to you, *bobonne?*"

The woman shook her head slowly. "No . . . Unless— No, he's shorter than medium and I never thought of him as plump."

"Who is this?"

"Monsieur Auger. He lives in a villa in the new subdivision."

"Is he married?"

"Oh yes, to a very nice wife. Madame Auger is very pretty, very sweet—a homebody who almost never leaves Juvisy. *Tiens!* That reminds me——"

The three men looked at her expectantly.

"Yesterday while I was doing my laundry in the yard, I saw her walking toward the railway station. She must have been taking the four thirty-seven for Paris."

"She has dark hair, hasn't she? And carried a black leather handbag?"

"I can't tell you the color of her handbag but she was wearing a blue suit and a white blouse."

"What does Monsieur Auger do for a living?"

This time the woman turned to her husband.

"He sells postage stamps," the landlord said. "You've seen his name in the classified ads—*Stamps for Collectors*. An envelope of a thousand foreign stamps for so many francs. Five hundred assorted for so much. A mail-order business, C.O.D."

"Does he travel much?"

"He goes to Paris from time to time. On stamp business, I suppose. He always carries his little suitcase. Two or three times when his train was late he stopped in here for a cup of coffee or a split of Vichy."

It was too easy. This wasn't even an investigation any more. It was a day in the country, an outing enlivened by a laughing spring sun and an ever-increasing number of the cups that cheer. And yet Maigret's eyes sparkled as though he had already guessed that behind this apparently banal affair lay one of the most extraordinary human mysteries he had ever encountered in his long career.

They gave him the address of the Augers. The new subdivision was quite a distance away, near the Seine. Hundreds, perhaps thousands, of little villas had arisen there, each in its own little garden, some of stone, some of pink brick, others of blue or yellow stucco. The worst part of it was that the villas had names instead of numbers, and it took the two inspectors a long time to find the villa *Mon Repos*.

The taxi rolled along new streets lined with half-finished sidewalks and newly planted trees as skinny as skeletons. Vacant lots separated many of the houses. They had to ask their way several times. After a number of wrong addresses, they finally reached their goal: a pink villa with a blood-red roof. A curtain in the corner window stirred slightly as Maigret and Janvier got out of the taxi.

"Should I wait outside, Chief?"

"Maybe you'd better. I don't expect any trouble, though. As long as there is somebody home."

He found the tiny bell in the too new door. He heard the ring inside. Then he heard other sounds—whispering, footsteps, a door closing.

At last the street door opened. Standing before Maigret was the young woman of the Café des Ministères and the Escargot. She was wearing the same blue suit and white blouse she had worn the night before.

"I'm Inspector Maigret of the Police Judiciaire."

"I thought it might be the police. Come in."

He climbed a few steps. The stairway seemed to have just come from the carpenter's shop. So did all the woodwork. The plaster on the walls was scarcely dry.

"Come this way, please."

She signaled through a half-open door to someone Maigret could not see. Then she ushered the inspector into the living room—the corner room with the curtains that had stirred a moment ago. There was a sofa with brightly colored silk cushions, books, bric-a-brac. On a coffee table there was the noon edition of a Paris newspaper with the dead man's photograph staring from the front page.

"Please sit down. Am I allowed to offer you something to drink?"

"Thank you, no."

"I should have suspected that it wasn't done. My husband will be here in a moment. You needn't worry. He won't try to run away. His conscience is clear. However, he has not been well all morning. We took the first train home today. He has a heart condition. He had a slight attack when we got home. He's up and dressed now, though. He's shaving."

Maigret nodded. He had heard the water running in the bathroom. The walls were not very thick in the new subdivision. He smiled at Madame Auger. She was quite pretty, in a wholesome, middle-class way. And she was quite calm.

"You must have guessed that I was the one who killed my brother-in-law," she said. "It was high time. If I had not killed him, my husband would be dead today. And after all, Raymond is worth a hundred Ernests."

"Raymond is your husband?"

"For the last eight years. We have nothing to hide, Monsieur l'Inspecteur. I know that we should have gone to the police with the whole story last night. Raymond wanted to do it, but I wouldn't let him. Because of his heart condition, I wanted him to get over the first shock before facing added complications. And I knew you would come here sooner or later."

"You mentioned your brother-in-law a moment ago. His name is different from your husband's."

"Combarieu was the husband of my sister Marthe. He used to be quite a nice fellow. Perhaps a little mad . . ."

"One moment. May I smoke?"

"Please do. My husband doesn't smoke because of his heart, but tobacco doesn't bother me a bit."

"Where were you born?"

"In Melun. We were sisters, Marthe and I, twin sisters. My name is Isabelle. We looked so much alike when we were tots that my parents—they're both dead now—used to put different colored ribbons in our hair so they could tell us apart. Sometimes we would play a joke on them and change the ribbons."

"Which one of you married first?"

"We were married the same day. Combarieu used to work at the prefecture in Melun. Auger was an insurance broker. They knew each other because, as two bachelors, they used to eat in the same restaurant. My sister and I met them together, so we were married together. We even lived on the same street in Melun early in our marriage."

"During this time, Combarieu was still working at the prefecture and your husband was still in the insurance business?"

"Yes. But Auger was already interested in philately. He started his own stamp collection for pleasure, but he realized that stamps could be a lucrative business."

"What about Combarieu?"

"He was ambitious. He was impatient, and he was always short of money. He met a man just back from the colonies who gave him the idea of going to Africa and making his fortune there. He wanted my sister to go with him, but she refused. She had heard that the climate was very unhealthy, particularly for women."

"So he went alone?"

"Yes. He was gone for two years. He came back with his pockets bulging with money. But he spent it faster than he had made it. He had already begun to drink. When he was in his cups he would proclaim to the world that my husband was a mouse instead of a man. A real man, he used to say, would not spend his life selling insurance or postage stamps."

"He went back to Africa?"

"Yes, but the second trip was less successful. His letters were as boastful as ever, but reading between the lines we could feel that things were not going too well for him. Then two winters ago my sister Marthe died of pneumonia. We wrote the bad news to her husband, who began drinking more than ever to drown his grief.

"A little later my husband and I moved here to Juvisy. For a long time we had been wanting to build our own home, and live closer to Paris. My husband had discovered he could make a comfortable living with his stamp business and had given up his insurance connections completely."

She spoke slowly, quietly, weighing every word. She seemed to be listening to the sounds from the bathroom.

"Five months ago my brother-in-law returned here without a word of warning," she continued. "Our doorbell rang one night and when I opened the door, there he was, weaving drunk. He gave me a funny look, and without even saying hello, how are you, he sneered and said, 'Just as I suspected.'

"At that time I hadn't the slightest idea what he was talking about. He didn't look well, and from the way he was dressed, he didn't seem too prosperous. In other words, it was not the brilliant home-coming he had enjoyed before, even if he had not been so drunk.

"He came in and for a few minutes talked a lot of incoherent nonsense. Neither of us could make out what he meant. Suddenly he got up and said to my husband, 'You're not only a scoundrel but you're the king of scoundrels. Admit it, now.' Without another word he left. We had no idea where he went.

"A few weeks later he returned, still drunk. He said to me, 'Well, well, my little Marthe.' 'You know very well I'm not Marthe,' I told him; 'I'm Isabelle.' He put on his best sneer. 'We'll see about that someday, won't we?' he said. 'As for your black-guard of a husband who sells postage stamps——'

"I don't know if you understand what was happening, Monsieur l'Inspecteur, but we didn't at first. He wasn't crazy, exactly, al-though he certainly drank too much. But he had this fixed idea, which we were slow to grasp. For weeks we didn't understand his threatening gestures, his sardonic smiles, his insinuations. Then my husband began to get threats by mail. Just one phrase: *I'LL GET YOU YET.*'"

"In a word," Maigret interrupted quietly, "your brother-in-law Combarieu for one reason or another got it into his head that his wife was still alive and that it was Auger's wife who had died of pneumonia."

It was a startling idea: twin sisters so alike that their parents had to dress them differently to tell them apart . . . Combarieu far away in darkest Africa, learning that his wife was dead . . . imagining on his return—correctly or not—that there had been a switch, that it was Isabelle who had died and that his own wife Marthe had taken her place in Auger's bed.

Maigret's eyes were half closed as he considered the situation. He puffed more slowly on his pipe.

"Life has been a nightmare for us these past months," Madame Auger continued. "The menacing letters became more frequent. Combarieu would stagger in here at all hours of the day and night, draw his revolver, point it at my husband, then put it away again and laugh. 'No, not yet,' he would sneer. 'It would be too good for you.'

"Then he took a room here in town so that he could torment

us more often. He's as sly as a monkey, even when he's drunk. He knows very well what he is doing."

"He knew," Maigret corrected her.

"I'm sorry." She colored slightly. "You're right. He knew. And I don't think he was too anxious to get into trouble. That's why we felt fairly safe here. If he had killed Auger here in Juvisy, everybody would know that he was the murderer.

"My husband hardly dared leave the house. Yesterday, however, he had to go to Paris on business. I wanted to go along but he wouldn't hear of it. He took the first train out, the early express, hoping that Combarieu would still be sleeping off his wine and wouldn't see him leave, even though Combarieu had a room just opposite the railway station.

"He was wrong. In the afternoon he telephoned me to come to Paris and bring his pistol to a café on Boulevard Saint Germain.

"I could see that my husband had come to the end of his rope, that he wanted to settle things once and for all. He told me on the phone that he would not leave the café before closing time. I brought him his Browning. I also bought a revolver for myself. You must understand, Monsieur l'Inspecteur."

"I understand that you had made up your mind to shoot before your husband was shot. Right?"

"I swear to you that when I pressed the trigger, Combarieu was raising his gun to aim at my husband . . . That's all I have to say. I'll be glad to answer any questions you want to ask me."

"How is it that your handbag is still marked with the initial *M?*"

"Because the handbag used to belong to my sister. If Combarieu was right, if there really had been this switch he was talking about so much, don't you suppose I'd have made sure to change the initial?"

"In a word, you are enough in love with a man to——"

"I love my husband."

"I was going to say you are enough in love with a man, whether he is your husband or not, to——"

"But he *is* my husband!"

"You are enough in love with this man, meaning Auger, that you would commit murder to save his life or to prevent him from committing murder?"

"Yes," she said.

There was a faint noise at the door.

"Come in," she said.

At last Maigret cast eyes on the man who had been described so differently by so many witnesses—the man with the blue-black mustache, the patience of an angel, and the obstinacy of a mule. In his domestic setting he was a great disappointment. After the young woman's declaration of love the man impressed Maigret as despairingly commonplace, the very quintessence of mediocrity.

Auger looked about him uneasily.

The woman smiled and said, "Sit down. I've told the inspector everything . . . *Your heart?*"

Auger poked vaguely at his chest and said, "Seems all right."

A JURY in the Court of Assizes for the Department of the Seine found Madame Auger not guilty on grounds of legitimate self-defense.

Every time Maigret has told about the case, he has always concluded with an ironic: "And that's the whole story."

"Does that mean," someone will always ask, "that you have reservations?"

"It means nothing at all—except that it is not impossible for a very commonplace little man to inspire a very great love, a passion of heroic proportions, even if he has a weak heart and sells postage stamps for a living."

"What about Combarieu?"

"Well, what about him?"

"Was he crazy when he imagined that his wife was not dead at all but was passing herself off as Isabelle?"

Maigret would shrug and mockingly declaim:

"A very great love! A grand passion!"

And sometimes when he was in particularly good humor, perhaps sipping some fine old calvados that he had warmed gently by holding the inhaler between the palms of his hands, he would continue:

"Is it always the husband who inspires these great loves and mad passions? And don't sisters often have the grievous habit of swooning over the same man? Remember that Combarieu was far away . . ."

Then, puffing great clouds of smoke from his pipe, he would conclude:

"Too bad the parents were dead, so we couldn't question them about the twins who couldn't be told apart. Anyhow, it was a fine day—the most beautiful spring day I ever saw. And I doubt if I ever drank so much on any one case. If you catch Janvier in an unguarded moment, he might even tell you we were surprised to find ourselves singing duets in the taxi coming back to Paris. And Madame Maigret has always wondered why I had a bouquet of violets in my pocket when I got home. . . . What a Jezebel, that Marthe! Excuse me, I mean, that Isabelle!"

A1